CHRONICLES OF THE NINE ISLES

- THE LOST DRAGON -
- & -
-THE WIDOW OF ELLAMAR-

By
Paul Lewis Jr.
And
Deona Ray

Cover design by Amazon.com, Inc.

Printed by Amazon.com, Inc. in Middletown, DE. Made in the USA

First printing, September 2021.

Kindle Publishing
ISBN 9798470838483

TABLE OF CONTENTS

TABLE OF CONTENTS (continued)

DEDICATED TO
THE CHILDREN AND FACULTY
OF
EAST CHEATHAM ELEMENTARY SCHOOL

SPECIAL THANKS TO…
DEONA RAY
CYNTHIA VONDOHLEN
MELISSA JONES
LORI SPEICH
SUSAN COLLINS
BRENDA CRAIG
STEVEN WRIGHT
SUSAN PEARSON
ANGEL THOMAS
GWENDOLYN RIGSBY
CAROL LEWIS
AMANDA FORD
ANNALISA LEWIS
BRI SOGLA
AND
AMBER BLYSTONE

1
THE SISTERS OF DESTINY

The four sisters were gathered at a round table, upon it was a large sphere of ice held in place by a wooden stand. The surface of the ice was like glass, smooth and clear, but inside the frozen ball was a swirling mist.

The sister wearing the black cloak gazed hard at the orb. "It's time, dear sisters," she said, eagerly.

"Are you sure?" asked the shortest sister wearing the white cloak.

"Of course she is, and I know how to proceed." declared the sister in the purple cloak confidently.

"I see him now," said the final sister impulsively, wearing the cloak of blue. "He is the one I saw on the throne."

"Where is he now?" asked the sister in white.

The sister in purple studied the images in the mist carefully. "He is at a celebration."

"What of the dragon?" asked the sister in black.

"She is not at the celebration. She is in Dayle," the sister in purple said, confused why a dragon would be at a celebration with humans.

The sister in black glared at her sister in purple. "I know the dragon wouldn't be at the celebration."

"Sisters, may we continue?" asked the sister in white.

"We waste time bickering."

"She was the one jesting, not I," began the sister in black. "We have very little time. He must be in Dayle in five days!"

"He will be there in time," declared the sister in blue.

"Doesn't it tire you to know the end before the beginning all the time?" asked the sister in white of her sister in blue.

"Yes, it is terribly boring at times," replied the sister in blue.

"Enough of this babble," ordered the sister in black, who was obviously the one in charge. "We must begin our work."

"I agree," chimed the sister in purple. "I will set things into motion."

"Then do so sister, post haste!" chirped the sister in black anxiously.

2
ON THE EVE OF ALL THINGS

ONE

Rikter shifted in his seat again as the party going on around him filled his ears with conversation, laughter and song, as well as bombarding his eyes with colorful streamers, floating lanterns that held flittering firelight and dancing revelers. He didn't want to be there, and felt that such a raucous festival for him and his crewmates was over-embellished, to say the least. Regardless of his feelings, he had been ordered to attend by the captain of the ship he served on, so there he sat alone in the small dining hall, fulfilling his obligation.

As third officer of the merchant vessel, Leonora Ander, Rikter was the youngest ever to have such a rank, at sixteen years old. He was also one of the best sailors in all the Nine Isles. He loved sailing and the freedom of the sea. The spacious wide world was where he was most comfortable and anything smaller than that was like putting him in a box. That is why he disliked large parties in small dining halls because they were cramped and loud, and he did not enjoy cramped and loud places.

The festivities he was forced to attend were

a celebration of the last shipment of much needed supplies the Leonora Ander had delivered to the small harbor town of Braeggon before the winter. It was during those winters that Tarpor Bay would freeze and prevent any ships from sailing in, or out for the entire winter, and this year's freeze was imminent.

It was Rikter's first time in Braeggon, on the isle of Dameron, the southernmost realm of the Nine Isles. In his mind he pictured the town full of adventurers, explorers, and warriors, all using the village as a safe haven. He imagined it was where they ate and drank and told wild tales before heading out into the wilderness to seek fortune and glory again, a very romantic idea, but the truth was far more dull.

Braeggon was a town of hunters, farmers, fisherman, masons and families. No warriors, explorers or adventurers to be found anywhere. The sole purpose of the town was to provide for Blackhawk Deep, the capital.

Blackhawk Deep was surrounded by mountains where it rested atop a steep bluff overlooking Tarpor Bay. The land there was so rocky that the crops would not grow, and the livestock had nowhere to graze, so Blackhawk Deep relied on the supplies provided by Braeggon. In turn, Braeggon relied on the winter cargoes provided by ships like the Leonora Ander.

The one good quality of the tiny harbor port

that Rikter enjoyed was that it had soft beds, delicious goat cheese and the most succulent elk meat to be found anywhere. Still, Rikter did not care for large parties. He was easy to please and enjoyed simple pleasures. He also didn't care for being in one place too long, and the Leonora Ander had been docked for two days now. For him that was long enough.

He sighed longingly to be out on the water.

"What's going on in your head this time, Rikter?" said a friendly, heavy voice.

The young third officer looked up and saw his friend Brice sit across from him at the thick oak table. He was a barrel-chested brute of a man, and the heavy hide coat, fringed with fur around the collar, only made him look larger. In his hand was a large mug of ale-root with a thick foam sticking over the rim. He hadn't drunk any of it yet.

"Just thinking," Rikter told him.

Brice laughed through his bushy, red beard. "What thoughts are troubling you this time?"

"I'm eager to get back on the water, that's all," Rikter told him.

"I'm sure you are, my boy, but there is a time and place for such things! Now is the time to partake of our hosts hospitality!" Brice exploded merrily.

Rikter smiled to placate Brice. "Is it necessary?"

"Aye, boy! Necessary and polite! Now eat something, my boy, you're getting thin in the middle! I can see your ribs!" with that said he took a hefty drink from his ale. The foam stuck heavily to his lush beard, and he slapped the mug back to the table. He belched his approval.

"I did eat. I had the roast duck and potatoes," Rikter said.

"Very good! As did I!" Brice said. "Do me a favor lad, don't tell Thornsby, but his skills as a cook are pale by comparison with whomever conjured up this feast!"

Rikter chuckled back at him. "He will not hear that from me. How is the ale-root?"

"It's very good, but not better than the Thysarian blend we picked up in Ward a year ago," Brice said.

"I remember. I saw my first dwarf while we were docked there! They're taller than I expected," Rikter recollected.

"Aye, they are that, and strong as an ox! I wouldn't cross one on my best day!"

"When are we to leave?" Rikter asked suddenly, cutting through the fat of the conversation.

"That is what we are not going to discuss! I have something prepared for you, Rikter my boy!" Brice waved at a servant to bring a pitcher of buttered-honey milk. "I know you don't like the ale, so I arranged your favorite drink in the hopes it would lighten your mood."

A maiden hurried over to their table and placed the pitcher of buttered-honey milk next to Rikter's mug. "Would you like me to pour it for you?" she asked politely.

"No thank you," Rikter shook his head and she went back to work. He poured the warm buttered-honey milk into his mug and took a sip. It was good, probably the best he had ever tasted, and very similar to butterscotch.

Brice watched him then asked eagerly. "Well? How is it?"

"Very good," Rikter replied with a smile of satisfaction. "It's really good!"

"Brilliant!" Brice bellowed with glee. "And I see your sour face now smiles! My work here is done." He then swallowed the remainder of his ale and pushed himself upright from his chair. "Come, my boy! I challenge you to a game of darts!" He pointed toward the group of shipmates in a corner.

The idea of darts excited Rikter that he quickly forgot himself and after swallowing the rest of his drink he shot up like a bolt of lightning. "I'll take that challenge!"

As they headed over to the dartboard, Rikter caught a glimpse of a cloaked man entering the bustling hall carrying a small white bird. The man weaved through the patrons and stopped in front of Captain Leonora Jones as she was engaged in conversation with several of the town's provincial leaders.

"What's going on there, Brice?" Rikter jerked his head in the captain's direction.

Brice craned his head to look. His brow furrowed in thought. "Hmm, not sure, lad." His face lit up with the realization of an idea. "That could be our bonus receipt from Blackhawk Deep!"

Rikter nodded, slowly accepting Brice's explanation as possible fact, then taking a few darts from his friend, he turned to enjoy their game.

TWO

The cloaked man carrying the white bird, called an Avee, bowed his head slightly to Captain Leonora Jones before asking her. "Are you Captain Jones?"

Captain Jones' wide smile fled at the sight of the man and his small white friend. "I am," she replied. "What have you there young man?"

"Forgive the interruption, but a message has arrived for you and is of the utmost importance," the man responded earnestly. With his other hand he produced a small bit of rolled parchment and handed it to her.

Captain Jones nodded at him. "Thank you."

She unrolled the note as the messenger walked away. After reading the message she sighed with disappointment. "I apologize for the interruption, gentlemen," she said to her hosts. "Please excuse me I must speak to my crew. Thank you for your hospitality." After a few handshakes she walked deeper into the dining hall to find her first officer, Brice, playing darts with a few crewman and Rikter.

"Brice, Rikter, gather the crew and meet me at the wharf as soon as you can. I'll be there shortly," Captain Jones ordered urgently.

Before she could dart away Brice caught her arm with a hand, something only he could get away with, and asked. "Is there a problem, Captain?" He let her go when she looked at him sharply.

"Gather the crew to the wharf and I will join you shortly to explain. I have matters to attend to first, Mr. Brice." She pulled her arm free and hurried through the crowd and out into the chill of late autumn.

Brice and Rikter exchanged looks of confusion before carrying out the orders their captain had given them.

Captain Jones quickly walked along Middle Street, the soles of her polished black long boots echoing off the cobblestones and the dark, silent buildings around her. The chill of the night forced her to use her gold waist-sash as a scarf.

With each lamp she passed it felt as though the street were growing longer and longer. It was probably because time was against her ship and crew. The message she had been given was the culprit of her anxiety. The note had said something that she was certain was untrue, and it was luck that she was it Braeggon when she had received it. Anywhere else in the Nine Isles and she could avoid what the note had warned her about.

When she reached the end of the market district she went down a side street between a small hovel and a blacksmith stall. She continued along this street until she came upon an abandoned home with a thatched roof whose insides were mournfully dark. After a quick look to see if anyone was nearby, she reached into her long-coat and retrieved a small leather pouch.

Captain Jones untied the cord and took a pinch of the powder inside, then flicked it onto the marker stone near the steps to the front door. She then said, "From the fire in my heart, that compels me to roam, show me the way, to an old friend's home."

A gust of wind swept along the street and seemed to wrap itself around the withered door frame, tossing her golden trusses behind her as if she were flying among the clouds. The spell had worked.

She went to the finely carved door, whose

surface had once been splintered and decaying only a minute ago, and lifted the latch. The door swung open to a small room that was lit by a warm fire in the hearth. She went inside and closed the door behind her.

The room was very cozy and humbly decorated. Two couches and a brown thick rug claimed the middle of the room, while a small table and two chairs sat quietly in a corner near the hearth. Several knitted images stitched to thick leather hung on the walls and a shelf full of food-stuffs occupied the remainder of the room. A cooking pot hovered over the fire, full of a robust smelling soup whose aroma permeated the air around her. A doorway off to one side had candlelight flickering onto the floor and it seemed to be moving into the main room.

"Grimmholder?" she called softly.

"Leonora?" a kindly, old voice replied. "Is that you?"

"It is," she answered, delighted that her friend was awake at such a late hour.

From the other room a bald, and very old man inched his way through the doorway. His long white beard stretched below the braided cord tied around his waist. His clothes, a patchwork of different colored fabrics sewn together haphazardly, were dirty and stained. Draped over his shoulders was an old, gray cloak that dragged along the floor behind him. A single lit and melting candle crowned the top of a misshapen wooden staff he used as a walking stick. The wax from his source of light dripped and trailed along the twisted, gnarled length. Dotted all over the floor was dried candle wax from his movement in his home.

When he saw Captain Jones he smiled showing only a few teeth that he had left. "Leonora!" he chirped as he shuffled slowly toward her.

Captain Jones went to him, if only to ease his struggle to walk, and hugged the old man gently. His body in her arms felt like she was hugging a cloud.

"How long has it been?" Grimmholder asked.

"Fifteen years," she told him.

"Fifteen years! Goodness, has it been that long?" He gestured for her to sit at the table. "So tell me, how is Ander?"

Captain Jones sat down and her face became sullen. "I'm sorry to be the one to tell you, Grimm, but Ander died seven years ago."

Grimmholder felt his heart shudder at those words. "Oh, Leonora, that is unfortunate. He was a good man."

"And a good husband."

"How did it happen?" he asked as he fetched two cups and set them on the table, and with an outstretched hand a pitcher sailed from the shelf to his fingers. He poured gub-berry spirits into both cups.

Captain Jones again swallowed her pain and continued. This was not the time to dwell on lost love, and the faster she explained the better her chances of journeying to Ironshire without incident. "He was lost to the sea."

As she drew breath to explain the real reason she had come he said, "It wasn't the Great Storm was it? Has it been twenty five years since the last one already?"

"No…" she began, but again he cut her off.

"The sea is a most unruly and unpredictable monster. The water behaves most foolishly, it seems to me, and without remorse when it takes a sailor to the bottom! For all the magic I have, no spell can I conceive will affect the sea. I've tried, dear lady! Oh how I have tried to force the sea to do as I command but I have yet…"

"Grimm…"

He continued without pause, "…to witness success against such a creature as the sea! I have sought counsel from other mages, sorcerers, and warlocks, but none know how to tame it with our craft…"

"Grimm!" Captain Jones snapped loudly.

It seemed to be enough to regain his attention and he gazed at her intently. "Yes, Leonora?"

"My coming here was not simply a social

reason. I have need of your wisdom."

Grimmholder's craggy smile decorated his friendly face. "By all means, what is it you need?"

"I am sorry that I don't have the proper time to give you. I received this message tonight at the town dining hall. It was carried by a white Avee." She handed Grimmholder the parchment.

He sat across from her at the table. "A white Avee, you say. Are you certain?"

"Yes, Grimm."

"Then it must be very important, or very dire," he pondered aloud.

"Please, Grimm, time is very short," she implored.

"Of course." With his withered hands, he lifted the note to his eyes and read it. "Hmm," he began. "Ahh, the Ring of Light has been seen!"

"Yes," agreed Captain Jones. "But that cannot be! Its only been nine years since the last one!"

Grimmholder nodded as he read the message to its conclusion. He handed the parchment back to her. "Nine years, you say? That is interesting."

"Yes, to say the least. Could the observatory at High Point be wrong?"

"I don't believe so. The message is very clear and a large storm was seen by the lighthouse in Grayvale, where this parchment was relayed to you," Grimmholder surmised.

"Yes, but is it the Great Storm?" Captain

Jones pleaded. She needed him to answer and the answer she was hoping for was 'no it is not the Great Storm'.

"If the Ring of Light was indeed in the skies above High Point, then the Great Storm is upon the sea tonight," Grimmholder told her, and he knew it was not what she wanted to hear. He was also curious. "Why does this news disturb you?"

Captain Jones met his gaze and a tear slipped free and slid down a cheek. "Because I'm in command of The Leonora."

"Ahh, and how is the old girl?"

Captain Jones tried to smile, but only managed to grimace. "She's a fine ship. I renamed her."

"And what name did you give her?"

"I added Ander's name to the end. The Leonora Ander."

Grimmholder again beamed at her, then placed a warm comforting hand on hers. "It is a very fine name you have given her."

She managed to return his smile, and somehow it warmed her lonely heart.

THREE

Captain Jones wasted no time in threading her way along the cool, nearly deserted streets of Braeggon in haste to reach the wharf and her crew.

Her footfalls were quick and with purpose. A park she hurried through would have been enjoyable if not for the late hour, but in the dim moonlight she could still see the brown and orange leaves clinging to their branches and peppering the stone under her feet.

When she emerged from a side street onto the avenue by the wharf she could see her crew, only a mere eighteen men and women, huddled together under an oil-lamp muttering to each other. Most likely they were confused by their departure from the festivities.

She hurried toward them as Brice and Rikter turned to meet her. She spoke quickly, "Brice, how long will it take us to leave the bay?"

Brice returned her question with a slack-jaw. "Captain?"

Rikter chimed in for his friend. "Three days if we leave tonight, Captain."

"Aye," Brice agreed.

"Did you explain to the Steward of Braeggon that we had to depart?"

"Aye, I did. With your deepest regrets, Captain."

"Thank you, Mr. Brice. Then we leave now. Make the ship ready to sail within the hour, gentlemen. We have precious little time," Captain Jones told them sternly and she rushed onto the docks where the Leonora Ander was berthed.

The ship was of a design called a galleon.

Normally a galleon is very tall above the waterline and long from bow to stern, but the Leonora Ander was shorter and slimmer. When she was built, Ander Jones had asked that the ship be more narrow so that the hull would slice through the water and be faster than most galleons. Which the ship was and gained a reputation for being the fastest, and smallest, galleon on the seas in the Nine Isles. Unfortunately she was also the only galleon that could not carry as much as her larger 'sisters' could. The ship boasted two masts whose main sails were dyed the most beautiful shade of blue.

Tonight, Captain Jones' ship would have to be faster than it had ever been.

"Aye! You heard your captain!" Brice barked to the crew. "Make haste and ready the ship!"

The crew immediately hastened across the gang-plank and onto the ship. They scattered across the deck like busy ants, climbing the netting called shrouds to reach the sails that were tied to the main yard and topsail yard; crossbeams at the mid and high points on the main and mizzen masts. Others secured the four small cannons to the deck and stowed some cargo that they would need for the voyage home. Among these stocks was cargo bound for Ironshire, worth a small fortune, that they were lucky to acquire a day ago when they arrived in Braeggon.

Brice turned to Captain Jones as she and Rikter stepped onto the Leonora Ander's deck behind him. "Captain, is it too much to be asking the reason for our early departure?"

Captain Jones took a moment to scan around them for a curious ear, but the crew were too engaged in their work to hear. "Very well, Mr. Brice, but this must stay between the three of us. Am I to be understood accordingly?"

"Always Captain, you have my word," Brice said.

"Of course, Captain. You have my word as well," said Rikter.

Captain Jones took a deep breath to calm her nerves then began. "I received news by messenger from Grayvale. The Ring of Light was seen eight days ago, and a storm was spotted east of Durden in Ellamar just four days ago. The watchmen at the Lighthouse of Durden believe it to be the Great Storm."

"That's impossible!" Brice exclaimed. "It has been only nine years since!"

"We're at least a sixteen days from East Hold. Is that enough time to get to Ironshire before it passes?" Rikter asked.

"No way of knowing, my boy. The winds here have been strange since we arrived," Brice said.

"Could it be an omen?" Rikter surmised, then regretted the statement too late.

Captain Jones glared at her third officer. "Mr. Rikter, you understand that I will have no talk aboard this ship of omens!"

"Yes Captain. My apologies," Rikter uttered.

"Don't you have duties to attend to, mister?" she asked, sending him on his way. As soon as he had gone she turned to tour the ship with Brice on her heels. "Tell me Mr. Brice, what are your thoughts about young Rikter?'

"He's a very good sailor, Captain. He is at home on the seas and works harder than most of the crew. You couldn't ask for a more determined soul and loyal third mate."

"I'm going to hold you to that," she told him, looking upward at the Leonora Ander's colors crowning the main masthead. The flag was barely fluttering in the light breeze against the blackness of the night sky dotted with tiny pinpoints of starlight. The lazy flag bothered her. "The winds here are stranger than they have been in years past."

Brice looked up at the Leonora Ander's colors, a white hawk on a field of maroon, the edges trimmed in gold as it hung overhead. "It doesn't bode well, Captain."

A crewman mid-ship shouted toward them. "Ready to shove off, Captain!"

Captain Jones and Brice took their posts on the bridge above the captains quarters at the aft of the ship, while eight of the crew dashed below deck to man the mooring oars. They began to row the ship away from the docks and out of the harbor. The remainder of the crew released the sails, took the slack from the rigging and tied them off. The light gusts of wind lazily filled the sails but offered very little help in moving the ship.

Just when Captain Jones was about to curse the Divine of the weather, a powerful wind picked up and the ship was on her way. Leonora Ander's sails ballooned to their capacity, rocketing her out of the harbor and into open waters of Tarpor Bay without much help from the rowers. The forward keel cut through the icy water as easily as a sharp knife cleaved through butter.

"Tell the rowers to stop!" Captain Jones called out to a crewman below. "We have the wind!"

"We have the luck of a Divine somewhere!" Brice declared excitedly.

"It appears so. We may beat the ice if this wind holds," Captain Jones surmised. All her hopes of reaching Ironshire ahead of the mysterious storm seemed to be dependant upon luck, and deep in her heart she feared it would not be enough.

FOUR

Rikter made his way to the galley after

meticulously applying a putty he had made himself to seal a few small leaks in the hull. If they were racing to get ahead of a potential storm he wanted to make certain that the ship could absorb the pounding. In only a few hours the putty would be as hard as wood. Once he had finished that hour-long task he went to the cargo hold to inspect the ties securing the crates there. Satisfied that the crew had done the job correctly he climbed the steps to the galley and found an empty spot on one of the benches at a table.

Around him the crew went about some of the more mundane tasks now that the serious work had been done. He reached for a clay pitcher of water, filled a mug to the rim and chugged it down.

He thought about what the captain said about the Great Storm. Was that destructive calamity really what the watchmen in Durden had seen? If so, he was both eager to witness it and a little frightened as well.

The last time the Great Storm had been through he was but seven years old and living with his mother in a storeroom of a mercantile in Ironshire. He never attended schools, so what little he did know about the world he learned from customers and passers-by on the street. Most of what he heard were from the mouths of sailors, and as a result he was very learned about the creatures of the sea and the legends that went with them.

When he was eleven his mother had passed on and he took a job with the owner of the mercantile in exchange for being allowed to live in the storeroom, alone. It was while he was there that he met Captain Jones. She had come in to purchase provisions for the ship and crew when he was twelve. From the look of her clothes he knew she was a ship's captain, and he hounded her for a chance to be a crewman on her ship. She told him under no terms would she take on a child to serve on her ship.

Captain Jones told him this for two more years. Each time she visited he pressed her for a chance to serve. When he turned fourteen, she finally gave in and made him the ship's cabin boy.

His first year aboard was a struggle for him. First of all he was seasick…A LOT. Then when he experienced the first rough seas of his new career, he found it difficult to stay upright. He fell…A LOT. Lastly he wasn't able to sleep at sea as the rocking kept him awake, so he slept whenever he could when he was supposed to be doing his duties. He got in trouble…A LOT.

When he became accustomed to life on the water, which took him a year, and he never complained, he began to enjoy his new life. He had learned more in that time than when he was in Ironshire. The crew taught him how to tie a large assortment of knots and how to use a lead line; a knotted rope for measuring depth. He quickly learned about the ship's rigging and how to furl and unfurl the sails, and what each was called. He also was taught the benefits of hard work, and on the Leonora Ander he worked very hard.

Everyday Rikter had to wash the dishes for the cook, Thornsby, after breakfast, then swab each deck. Afterwards he would wipe every bit of iron in the ship with an oil called ulen, to prevent rust from forming. By the time he was done with that it would be time for lunch, and again he would have to wash those dishes too. Rats onboard also provided him with another task, removal of the rodents by any means he could try. It was while performing this job that he discovered he had a talent for crafting, and made a rat trap that captured rather than killed them.

Then, when he turned sixteen, three months ago, he had finally earned Captain Jones' respect, because she had promoted him to third officer. With their return to Ironshire he would do so as an officer of a ship and not a stock boy. The thought excited him.

If they managed to beat the storm to the Iron Channel separating Dameron from East Hold, he would get to see Ironshire for the first time in just over a year.

Brice suddenly planted his girth next to Rikter as he drank another mug of water. "I have good news, Rikter. The winds picked up while you were below and we are making good time."

Rikter nodded, relieved to hear what his friend had to say. "That is excellent news. What about the captain? Is she still upset with me?"

Brice filled a mug with the water pitcher and drank before saying, "I don't know, but she did ask me what I thought of you."

"What did you tell her?" he asked.

"I told her that if you didn't fall overboard, you must be useful somewhere," Brice joked, laughing heartily.

Rikter laughed. "No, really, what did she say?"

"Nothing that you should concern yourself with. Now tell me how the is the ship? Are we prepared for rough water?"

"Aye, sir. The cargo is secure and there are no leaks in the hull."

"That is good news, my boy! Did you have to use your putty on the hull?" asked Brice.

"In a few places, so we're watertight, Brice."

"I suppose, Mr. Waycross, as third officer, you should go and report that to the captain."

Rikter's mouth fell open a moment. "You want me to do that?"

"I do." Brice began. "So get to it!"

Rikter bounded to his feet. "Aye sir," he stammered as he dashed up to the main deck, and onto the quarterdeck where Captain Jones was at the helm. He gasped for air while she waited for him to speak.

"Have you something to report, Mr. Rikter?" Captain Jones asked him. She wanted to grin but held back.

"Mr. Brice ordered me to report ship's status, Captain."

"Status, mister?" asked Captain Jones.

"Ship is secure, Captain," he answered proudly.

Captain Jones nodded to him. "Very good, Mr. Waycross. Have you anything to eat yet?"

"No, Captain."

"Then get something in your belly, Mr. Rikter. You have third watch and will man the helm tonight," she told him, knowing that he would appreciate the responsibility and the challenge.

Rikter felt a sensation overwhelm him that could only be elation. "Aye, aye, Captain!" he sputtered with excitement, then returned to the galley for a quick supper.

3
A FALLEN LORD

ONE

Stretching into the sky, almost touching the clouds themselves, loomed the impressive pearl-colored stone tower of the royal palace overlooking the sprawling city of Skyvale, the capitol of the isle of Ellamar. Dwarfing the palace, a mere mile to the north west, sat an enormous snow-capped mountain covered with evergreen trees. The people of Ellamar called it Mount Immanis, and it was the second largest mountain in the realm.

The city of Skyvale was one of the largest cities in all the Nine Isles, second only to Stoval on the isle of Revelstoke in the west. At the center of this bustling metropolis was the almost as imposing royal palace. The granite that the palace and walls around it was built from was smooth as glass and could be seen from miles outside the city.

Beautiful gardens and courtyards filled the space between the walls and the rounded palace that narrowed the higher it reached into the sky. Numerous balconies and open verandas dotted the surface of the tower, providing a three hundred and sixty degree view of the entire city. Great, thick ropes were anchored into four sides of the rounded tower, and stretched outward where they were attached to recessed stanchions in four of the wall towers.

Hundreds of royal guards, their white and blue armor glinting in the sunlight, patrolled the ramparts on the walls, the gardens below and many of the balconies on the tower.

To the southeast of the palace was a great expanse of blue called Skyvale Fjord, that began at the city's wharf market and disappeared into the western horizon. Hundreds of sailing ships plowed the waterway between the north and south banks. Rocky, unforgiving mountains dominated both shorelines like unmoving gray giants, whose tops were capped with crystalline white snow all year long. They had been named the Cahannel Mountains.

Hundreds of years ago, during the age of humankind called the Reign of the Kings, Skyvale was the capitol of the Nine Isles, but now it was simply the capitol of Ellamar. It was during that time that an age of peace existed between all the Lord Regents, and it that lasted for generations…until the dragons of the world vanished.

Since that time each province was run by Lord Regents and their heirs, and their heir's heirs, and so on and so forth. Bickering between regents soon escalated to hostility, then violence and lastly warfare. To this day only four Lord Regents ruled the realms, and of those only the elves and dwarves were at arms over the isle of Elsemere, while a delicate peace existed between the others.

Lady Samarra Baylen, wife of the Lord Regent of Ellamar, admired the view of the sunrise from the terrace in her sitting room. She had just awoke and slipped into her warmest robe so she could hurry to the terrace where she normally ate breakfast while watching the morning sun peak over the Cahannel Mountains. Most mornings her husband, Greggory Baylen, fifteenth lord of the House of Baylen, would've been with her on the terrace, but he still hadn't retuned from handling a dispute between two villages in the north. It was the thirtieth day since he had left with a small regiment of knights.

Servants quietly came into the room pushing a cart with her breakfast and placed the plates of food onto a polished wooden table on the terrace. Fried eggs, a bit of cheese and butter, bread and salted pork along with a pitcher of fresh milk was laid in front of her. The smells from it all pleased her very much. She thanked the servants and dismissed them before taking a bite from the warm bread.

How she wished Greggory was there. She missed her morning kiss from him and his bushy mustache tickling her nose. Worrying about him was something she didn't do. He was a wonderful diplomat and an excellent swordsman and the men with him were the very best in all of Ellamar.

She wondered what he was doing right now, so far away, and managed to smile at the thought of him jesting with his most trusted knights. For the men, jesting was how they relaxed. Although raucous, it seemed to help their moods.

Lost in the thought, Lady Samarra was snatched back into reality by the loud, metallic clanging of the King's Bell on one of the smaller towers in the palace walls. It signaled the return of the king from long journeys.

"Greggory! He's back!" she cried then leapt from her chair, cinched the robe tightly and ran out of the terrace room and straight toward the lift; a mechanized wonder of an invention that allowed travel up and down in the palace tower without the use of stairs. It used weights and counter-weights to work its magic.

The carriage Lady Samarra stepped into was made of fine polished oak and a wrought iron cage. The whole thing traveled through a vertical shaft and running the length of it was a bronze tube that connected at each floor to a small mouth-sized tube. The tubing was used to call to an operator at the bottom who would turn a valve on a water-wheel driven gear and move one of two levers to make the whole contraption work.

A servant closed the gates behind her and called into the tube. "Lady Samarra! Ground floor!"

A voice echoed back, "Ground floor!"

The rigging holding the cage rattled and it gently slid downward in the shaft until she was at the bottom where another servant opened the gates and she bolted across the spacious greeting hall.

Her heart was hammering in her chest with child-like enthusiasm as she squeezed through the large brass doors that were still being opened for her by two burly guards. The crisp morning air bit her when she crossed into the shadow of the granite walls to greet her husband. He was leading forty knights on horseback through the main garden with a few horse-drawn wagons trailing behind carrying their supplies and gear. Their armor had been cleaned and polished before they reached the city so they could make a grand return.

Lord Greggory, a large man with full cheeks, piercing green eyes that shined like emeralds and blazing red hair, lead the procession right up to the Grand Fountain before saying, "Hold!" His voice boomed like thunder and the entire procession halted immediately.

The Lord Regent of Ellamar swung an armored leg from around his horse and dropped to the ground. He looked toward his wife as she sprinted at him, a smile on her face from ear to ear. She leapt into his arms despite the plate-mail armor and planted a kiss on his fat lips.

"I've missed you!" Lady Samarra exclaimed.

"And I you, dear wife," he replied.

"I trust that your trip was well worth your time away from me?" she asked, half joking with him.

"It was, my wife. The northern people will not spill blood this winter, or any winter in the future," he declared, then spun to address his men. "Knights! You are dismissed for three days! Go to your homes and be with your families! My servants will handle the supply wagons and gear!" he told his weary men and each saluted with a fist over their hearts and rode away.

A squire took Lord Greggory's horse by the reins and led the equine away to the stables.

"So, my husband, how long will you stay this time?" Lady Samarra teased.

"Forever of course," he said as they both walked toward the palace.

"Why don't I believe you?"

"Your majesty, welcome home," a voice belonging to the palace steward greeted him when they were near the steps to the doors of the palace.

"Rafferty, thank you but I am no king so do not tie that title to my person," Lord Greggory said.

"Of course, my lord," Rafferty said.

"That's more appropriate. Now have someone see to the wagons and gear."

"At once, my lord," Rafferty said.

Lord Greggory and Lady Samarra went through the doors into the greeting hall where a small contingent of house servants waited patiently. They set to work helping him remove his armor, starting with the tapered half-kilt hanging from his right hip that covered his leg. When they had finished taking each piece of armor all he wore was a tunic and breeches and his boots.

"Ahh, I'm so relieved to be rid of that metal skin," Lord Greggory sighed with relief. "Am I too late for breakfast with my lady?" he asked.

"No, my lord, you are not. Your timing could not have been better," Lady Samarra told him, taking his arm with hers. They walked to the lift and rode it to the breakfast terrace with Rafferty behind them, and disembarked on their desired floor.

Rafferty looked to a kitchen server waiting by the doorway and instructed him to fetch breakfast for Lord Greggory. "Your breakfast is being prepared, my lord."

"Very good, Rafferty, thank you," Lord Greggory said.

"Before you sit, my lord, Hildegrinnel has requested an audience with you," Rafferty said.

"Can she not wait till after breakfast?" Lady Samarra asked.

A radiant white light burned into existence behind Rafferty, filling the room with its soft glow, and hundreds of orange-winged butterflies seemed to flutter into the room from within. Left standing where the strange event occurred was a short elderly woman with long white hair and wide, blue eyes. A thick white frilled cloak hung from her frail shoulders and nearly touched the floor. Small butterflies danced in the air around her when she moved about as though they were tied to her by string. Thin, wrinkled fingers clung to a twisted, ivory colored staff that was nearly twice her height. Growing out of the shaft was a leafy green vine that twisted from a point above her grasp to the top where a thumb-sized maple tree was rooted.

"Good morning, Hildegrinnel," Lord Greggory greeted her politely.

"Lord Greggory. It is agreeable to see you returned from the north unharmed," she declared.

"That was quite an entrance," Lady Samarra complimented.

"Thank you, my lady," Hildegrinnel replied. "My lord, it is urgent that we speak at once."

"Urgent, you say? What does this concern, wizard?" Lord Greggory asked.

"She's a witch, Greggory," Lady Samarra whispered in his ear.

"Witch it is," Lord Greggory said.

"Rafferty," Hildegrinnel said. "Leave me with the lord and lady."

Rafferty turned and left the room without a

word, leaving only the two royal guards behind.

"Now Hildegrinnel, what is so dire that you would interrupt my husband's precious time with his wife?" Lady Samarra asked with arms crossed.

"I fear that he, and my lady, are in grave danger." Hildegrinnel told them.

"Is that all?" Lord Greggory mocked. "You wizards and witches are always spouting warnings of danger. As the ruler of Ellamar I am constantly at risk. Am I not?"

"Yes, of course, but I fear this time may be different," Hildegrinnel said.

"In what way, Hildegrinnel?" Lady Samarra asked her.

Hildegrinnel's eyes fell to the floor. "The visions I saw in my crystal were of death."

Lady Samarra and Lord Greggory exchanged looks of concern. Hildegrinnel never before had visions of death, and for her to be doing so was very unusual.

"Whose death?" Lady Samarra asked fearfully. The pit of her stomach was starting to twist and knot.

"Lord Greggory's."

TWO

The kitchen server Rafferty sent away to fetch Lord Greggory's breakfast, briskly hurried down the polished marble hallway from the terrace room to the kitchen; one of fifteen in the palace; and went inside.

He wasn't just there to simply fetch Lord Greggory's breakfast. His task was much darker and deadlier.

He was here to change destiny itself.

He had no desire to be a servant living and working in the Royal Palace no matter how comfortable it would be to do so. He had no loyalty to the Lord Regent, Lady Samarra or anyone else in Skyvale. The thought of it all was unacceptable. His loyalty was to gold, and how much he could put into his coin purse.

Furiously chopping vegetables for a lunch stew was one of the thirty cooks that ran this particular kitchen. The other cook was butchering a small animal carcass, that looked to the servant like a pig, on a large table.

Three big brick fire pits were in the far wall with fat black pots hanging over their fires. Each one was filled with a delicious smelling concoction whose aroma filled the room and overwhelmed the senses.

In the center of the room was a large rectangular table with an assortment cooking utensils, plates, platters, bottles of spices and oils scattered across the surface. At one end was an oval plate with silver trim around the edges. On it was a hunk of butter and bread, some cheese, and a portion of cooked, spiced meat and fried eggs. A tall glass goblet filled with rose-berry mead sat next to it. The Lord Regent's breakfast.

The kitchen server went to the oval plate, making certain to keep his back to both cooks, and reached into a pouch inside his tunic to retrieve a small vial of black liquid. He looked over a shoulder for good measure, then pulled the tiny cork from the vial. A tendril of black vapor crept from inside and evaporated into the air as he gingerly tilted the edge over the glass goblet. Three drops of the liquid fell into the rose-berry mead and dissolved away. He then dripped four drops onto the spiced meat before replacing the cork onto the vial.

"Hey!" called one of the cooks. "What are you doing there?"

The server spun around nervously and hid the vial in the pocket of his breeches. "I was sent to get Lord Greggory's breakfast," he stammered.

The cook stepped away from chopping vegetables and came toward the server. "Well, you found it," he began gruffly. "So take it and go!"

"Yes sir," the server sputtered. He took the plate and turned to leave.

"Server!" the cook growled and it sent a wave of worry through the server's spine.

The server spun toward the cook. A bead of sweat trickled down the side of his face as the tension slowly mounted. "Yes," he mumbled.

"You forgot the rose-berry mead!" The cook pointed at the goblet.

Smiling apprehensively, the server retrieved the goblet and hurried from the kitchen.

The cook went back to his work, shaking his head with impatient frustration.

THREE

Lord Greggory hesitated only a moment, then grinned wryly. "Death takes all of us, Hildegrinnel. Why should I be no different?" he declared.

Lady Samarra nudged her husband with an elbow and jerked her head toward the elderly witch.

Lord Greggory's eyes looked over Hildegrinnel a moment, then he understood. The witch was hundreds of years old, although most wizards were, and no one was quite sure how long they lived. As a matter of fact, not one gravestone had ever been laid for a wizard that he knew of.

"Death takes *almost* everyone," Lord Greggory corrected. "When my time comes I cannot avoid it."

"Even if that time is today?" Hildegrinnel asked.

"Is it today?" Lady Samarra asked

desperately.

"I do not know, my lady. My magic comes from a source of life, and the vision I witnessed, comes from a dark place," Hildegrinnel said. "In months past I have become aware of a growing evil all around us. Its reach is long and wide over the Nine Isles."

"Then we should not speak of it anymore," Lord Greggory declared. "Lest we give this evil you speak of more reason to manifest."

At that moment the server came into the room with Lord Greggory's breakfast and mead. He hesitated a moment when all eyes had turned on him. "Your breakfast, Lord Baylen," he stammered.

"Ah, on the table if you wouldn't mind," Lord Greggory said. "Hildegrinnel, we will discuss this after I've had breakfast with my lady."

"As you wish, my lord," Hildegrinnel conceded and slowly hobbled toward the door.

The server placed the plate and goblet onto the table and hurried from the room ahead of the old witch.

Lord Greggory held a chair for Lady Samarra to sit, then took his place across from her. Her face still held concern for him because of the things Hildegrinnel had said.

"Greggory, shouldn't we take precautions about this?" Lady Samarra pleaded.

"Samarra, I see no reason to do so. The people of Ellamar have no quarrel with how I rule, or they would make themselves heard if it were so."

"But, my love, my life would be over if something…"

"Samarra, can we not discuss this later? As I said before, I would like to enjoy the morning with you," he said, reaching out to take her trembling hand with his.

She nodded reluctantly and took a sip from her cup of milk.

Lord Greggory smiled back at her and looked over his morning meal. The smell of the spiced meat and eggs made his mouth water. He scooped some eggs onto the spoon and hungrily swallowed them down before then reaching for his goblet of rose-berry mead. "The eggs are very good," he said. Then he placed the rim of the glass goblet against his lips and drank from it.

He nodded approvingly at Lady Samarra who stared back at him, her mouth agape.

"What is it, my dear?" Lord Greggory asked.

"Greggory, your lips have turned black!" Lady Samarra screamed.

Lord Greggory grinned with amusement. "Are you joking?" he asked, taking his spoon to use the polished silver as a mirror.

His lips had indeed turned a shade of black, and the sickly color began to spread like spilled ink on paper. Then a pain in his chest took his breath away, and clutching his heart he managed to gasp, "Oh my."

He fell from his chair, knocking the goblet he drank from to the floor, and went silent forever. Every inch of his skin had turned black as night.

"Hildegrinnel!" Lady Samarra shrieked as she scampered to Lord Greggory and dragged him onto her lap where she held him in her arms. "Hildegrinnel, what is happening to him?!" She cried hysterically.

The old witch spun around and rushed as quickly as she could toward Lord Greggory and Lady Samarra. Behind her several Royal Guards stormed in and surrounded the lord and lady after hearing the scream. Rafferty rushed in and knelt to Lord Greggory.

"What has happened?" he demanded, but Lady Samarra was crying too much to answer. He looked at the breakfast plate, then the goblet on the floor. He picked up the goblet and looked it over. Some of the mead was still inside.

"Poisoned?" he asked holding it toward Hildegrinnel when she was close.

Hildegrinnel eyed it closely. She muttered something too low for any one to hear and one of the butterflies flew into the goblet and landed inside. It tasted the liquid and the orange wings on its back suddenly turned white. She grimaced. "Ice-root poison."

Lady Samarra looked at both of them desperately. "Who, who would poison him? Why…" she growled, then a thought struck her dumb. "The server!" She jerked her head looking for the man who had brought Lord Greggory his breakfast. "Find him!" she barked.

Hildegrinnel raised her staff and brought it down quickly, striking the floor with a loud clack. A shockwave of her magic rocketed through the palace and the city like the boom of mighty thunder, rattling every window, shutter, floorboard, and rafter. Each guard heard the voice of the witch call for them to find the server at once.

"Find the servant who has killed your lord, Greggory Baylen, with poison! You will know his face from my mind's eye, and you will not kill him!"

"Fear not, Lady Samarra, the guards of the palace and city shall find and apprehend this assassin!" Hildegrinnel promised the Widow of Ellamar.

FOUR

The server, who was more assassin than servant, swiftly descended the long spiral shaft of stairs. His task had been completed, as far as he knew. There wasn't any doubt that Lord Greggory would die either from the spiced meat or the mead, it was simply a matter of time. All he needed to do was get out of the palace and make his way to the wharf where a boat was waiting to take him to Southfall, a port town by the Sea of Ellamar. It would be there that his master's ship would aid his escape.

The whole of the tower suddenly shuddered like the world was being shaken by an angry giant. The assassin leaned against the wall until the shaking stopped.

What was that? He thought.

Excited voices from guards several floors above told him that Lord Greggory had died from the poison and most likely they would be searching for him very soon. He no longer had time to be careful in making his escape.

He quickened his pace and emerged three floors below.

There weren't any guards when he stepped from the stairwell and hurried across the marble floor into a room with a balcony. He went to the rail and examined where he was. On the left, only twelve feet from the balcony was one of the great support ropes for the palace tower. It would take him an hour to climb along it to the wall below. He would need a faster way to traverse its length.

He examined the room he was in. It was filled with baskets and shelves of yarn, cloth and knitting needles and spinning wheels. An assortment of thick braided cords, rolled into bundles, hung on the walls.

He snatched one of the bundles, produced a small knife from his tunic, and cut a length of it. He then forced one of the spinning wheels free from its support and tied the cord onto one end of the wheel axle.

As he carried the wheel onto the balcony loud footsteps out in the halls alerted him. He dropped the contraption and rushed to the door. Using a stool he wedged it through the door latch and the door frame. No sooner had he done that the door trembled from a guard outside trying to open it.

"Is anyone in there? Open the door on the order of the Lady Samarra!" a heavy voice demanded.

The assassin quietly moved away from the door and went back to the balcony. Unfortunately, he bumped a spinning wheel and it fell over with a loud crash.

The voice at he door shouted in response. "Whoever is in there, open this door immediately!" Then the door buckled violently.

The guards were trying to break the door down and the thin leg of the stool would not hold long. The assassin forgot himself and grabbed the wheel before launching himself over the rail and toward the tree-trunk sized support rope. He desperately clutched the rope with one hand and dangled a moment until he was steady enough.

The door to the spinning wheel room shattered under the weight of several armored guards and they stormed into the room. Drawing their broadswords, they searched the room vigorously. A guard stepped onto the balcony and surveyed outside.

"The assassin is here! There!" he cried out and pointed at the assassin as he dangled by an arm from the support rope. "Call the archers to arms!"

A guard next to him raised a curved horn to his lips and blew into it. The horn blared out a note the archers would know.

The assassin managed to pull himself on top of the rope where he looped the cord below the support rope and tied it to the opposite axle of the spinning wheel. An arrow whizzed past his head, narrowly missing his left ear. He flinched and looked back.

Two floors up an archer was standing on a terrace with a bow. He notched another arrow and took aim, then let his arrow fly. Like the first it missed the assassin by only inches.

The Knight Sergeant; a knight higher in rank than a palace guard, but lesser than a Royal Knight; dashed onto the balcony. He looked at the assassin then to the terrace where the archer was preparing another arrow.

"Hold your fire! We need him alive!" the Knight Sergeant shouted to the archers.

The archer nodded his understanding and lowered his bow.

"You men, get down to the courtyard! Take him once he gets to the ground!"

The guards wasted no time in obeying their commander and rushed back through the room and to the lift.

There was no time to tighten the knots on the axle. The assassin took hold of the cord and slung himself below the rope. The spinning wheel strained under the weight, then began to roll along the length of the great rope downward with exceptional speed. The air whooshed past the assassin as he traveled toward the wall tower the support rope was attached to.

The assassin was traveling too fast to be able to stop and too high to fall safely. On the left and right he noticed numerous guards running on top of the wall to intercept him, each with a drawn sword and a scowl.

Moments before reaching the wall he realized there was a long reflecting pool below him. That was his chance! He let go of the cord and sailed downward through the air where he crashed into the water with a deafening splash. His backside bounced against the bottom of the pool. Surfacing, he scrambled through the water and climbed onto dry land, ignoring the ache in his bottom.

He quickly gauged his surroundings. The thick wooden doors of the gate to the city were still wide open and the portcullis; a cage-like wall of iron bars; hadn't been dropped. Angry guards, numbering at least fifty on one side, were clambering down the stone steps from the wall while another twenty burst from the palace greeting hall in full sprint at him.

The assassin ran as fast as his legs would carry him toward the gate, but with his clothes now damp and cold he wasn't as fast as he would've liked.

A guard shouted, "Close the gate! Close the gate!"

The gate operator on the wall slid a latch lock on a cog backward, then yanked a large lever to his breast. A great cylinder with a thick wound chain spun furiously and the portcullis began to drop to the ground.

The assassin closed in on the gate just as the portcullis slammed into the ground with a grand thud, but he leapt onto the bars and sprang from there to the frame of stones around the gateway. From there he climbed with such agility that there was no possibility he was a human. When he flipped onto the walkway of the wall the operator of the gate came at him with a studded club.

The operator swung the club at the assassin's chest in an attempt to knock the wind from him, but missed.

The assassin's body bent unnaturally around the wild club and he cart wheeled over it and off the wall into the city.

The operator stumbled and landed on a knee. He watched as the assassin landed on the roof of a small storehouse outside the palace, before dashing off and leaping a great distance to another rooftop.

"He's a serpine!" the operator yelled to the contingent of guards approaching the gate as he hurried to raise the portcullis.

The assassin easily hopped from rooftop to rooftop, covering nearly a dozen feet each leap. On the cobbled streets below city guards followed from building to building, using his shadow on the ground. The next jump was most unlucky, as a loose roof tile caused him to tumble over the edge and fall into a fruit cart.

The owner was a stout dwarf with a muscular build, black as pitch goggles and a long blond beard. He tossed the assassin into the street by the collar of his tunic into a crowd of onlookers.

"Argh, ya lousy hoodlums! You've wrecked me cart fer the last time with yer foolins!" he growled then grabbed a wooden hammer and swung it at the assassin, striking him across the back as he ran into an alley.

Wincing with pain, the assassin looked over

a shoulder at the dwarf who had given up chasing him, but three city guards took up the pursuit.

"He's in the alley heading for the harbor! Cut him off!" Shouted one of the guards and the last one ducked into a side street to try and get ahead.

A city guard jumped out from an alley and with his spear, tried to use the blunt end to strike him across the face. The assassin ducked the blow, somersaulted under a passing wagon drawn by an old ox, then dove into an open window of a house. The owners were in the middle of having their breakfast when the assassin ran past them and out their front door.

Once back on the street he wove his way quickly among the busy citizens, zigzagging the hustle and bustle. Soon fifteen city guards rushed onto the street and forced their way through the crowd. One of the guards spotted the assassin and called out.

"There he is!"

The assassin was growing tired of being chased. Spotting crates stacked near a high wall, he shoved aside several old women and sprinted onto them and dove over the wall. On the other side was another street populated with dozens of city guards marching quickly toward the docks several blocks ahead. The mass of citizens diverged to allow them to pass.

A captain, large for a man, spotted the

assassin and called out to his men. "There's the assassin! Take him into custody."

The assassin's face fell, but he was not finished yet. Two young guards were on him in a flash, but the Serpine suddenly became as sinewy as a snake. He dodged their attempts to wrestle with him and managed to slip under their legs. As he bolted away he stole a sword from one of their scabbards and slashed at the next three men who came for him. They fell to the cobblestone, dead.

He again sailed into the air, bounding off another guard's shoulders and upon returning to the ground he slid between the Captain's legs and continued fleeing into a narrow street. A dozen city guards gave chase, but he was too agile, and slipped through a wooden wall separating two alleys before they could see where he had gone.

He had finally lost them. They would have to go around four houses to catch him and he wasn't about to sit still for them to do so.

He snatched a tattered, smelly cloak hanging from an iron nail in a door frame to a house, and put it on. He pulled the hood over his head and casually reentered the street, easily blending in with the crowd.

A quick glance around told him the city guards hadn't made it to his side of the neighborhood yet. Ahead of him he could see the bell-post for the wharf.

Almost there, he thought.

As he got closer to the docks the number of pedestrians began to thin out and soon he could see the boat that was waiting to ferry him. He scanned behind him one last time and to his relief there still was not any guards.

The docks were busy with fisherman dropping off enormous loads of fresh fish, laborers loading and unloading goods from all over the Isles, and boats of all sizes bobbing with the moving water while they were moored.

On the furthest side was the boat he needed to be on. He casually made his way to the dock and as he stepped onto the wooden deck a brilliant light erupted in front of him followed by thousands of swarming butterflies. The air around him grew warm and smelled of strawberries.

Standing between him and the boat was Hildegrinnel, brandishing her staff with both of her withered hands, and a determined look about her face.

He stepped back, but held his ground. If he had to kill the witch to escape, then he would do so.

"You go no further, assassin," Hildegrinnel declared. She rapped her staff on the dock boards and again her magic moved the air. *"He is here with me at the docks, guards of Skyvale. Come quickly."*

"I am leaving this wretched city, witch, either around you or over your carcass," the assassin claim boasted. He took a step toward her, regardless of the sick feeling in the pit of his stomach that told him he was being foolish.

Hildegrinnel raised her staff and said, "Egroe!"

The earth beneath the assassin's feet grumbled as two white roots tore through cobblestone and twisted around his ankles like iron chains. He struggled to break free but was unsuccessful.

"I told you, assassin, you go no further," Hildegrinnel told him.

A city guard captain and four guards arrived and surrounded the assassin, their swords drawn and ready.

One of the guards was visibly angry. His sword hand was gripping the handle so tightly it had turned white, and he came forward intending to strike. "We should kill him now!" he growled.

"I agree," said another guard. "He has killed Lord Greggory and should die!"

The captain placed himself between his men and the assassin. "No! He is to be taken to the dungeon! Those are our orders, or did you forget your place and Lady Baylen's command?"

"But, captain, he has committed a crime punishable by death in the courts! Why do we not just quicken the execution by going through with it? He is guilty!" said the last guard. They were all very loyal to Lord Greggory and wanted retribution for killing their beloved benefactor.

"This is no place for revenge. We must exercise mercy and do as we were ordered. The courts will decide his fate," the captain said. He looked to the assassin. "Who commanded you to kill Lord Greggory?"

The assassin glared back at him. "It will do you no good to know. Your time in this world is at an end."

"What does that mean, assassin?" the captain demanded.

"The true king of the Nine Isles is returning," the assassin declared. "Nothing you do will stop it now that Lord Baylen is dead."

"The true king?" Hildegrinnel said, a feeling of darkness filled her with dread at his words. "Who is this true king?"

Thunder rumbled over their heads and they all looked to the sky. The sun had gone, hidden behind black clouds that came from nowhere, and the air had grown ice cold. A strong wind swept over the city and began to pick up speed, tearing the roof tiles from the homes and tossing the people of the city to the ground.

Hildegrinnel whirled her staff around her head and the air around them became still, but the wind continued to buffet Skyvale and her citizens.

"What is this dark weather?" asked the captain. His men had backed away from the assassin at his words and fear gripped them at the turn of the skies.

"I do not know, captain, but I believe he knows." Hildegrinnel said of the assassin. "Tell us who sent you, and you may yet live!"

"I will not speak," the assassin told her.

"That is true, my servant, you will not speak," said a thunderous voice in the sky, booming like the roar of a thousand lions.

"Master?" the assassin began, his voice cracking with fright.

The sky above them rumbled, then the clouds swirled and widened as if the whole of the world were trying to shatter. A blazing ring of fire wrapped around the rim of the vortex of dark clouds as it whirled with maddening hatred. Without warning, a column of the hottest, most untamable fire rocketed downward as if a star itself had been sent from the heavens to the earth. It raced directly at the assassin, who raised his arms for protection and screamed for help.

Hildegrinnel thrust her staff into the ground, and chanted, "Elitherandere!"

Just before the tower of fire reached them, millions of butterflies, shrouded in a warm glow, burst from the tiny tree on Hildegrinnel's staff, and formed a shield over them all. The pillar of fire struck the shield with a loud bang that shook their insides and made the very ground tremble throughout Skyvale. The buildings around then turned to ash and bolts of fire spilled off the butterfly shell that was their only protection.

Hildegrinnel spat through clenched teeth as she fought to maintain her magic spell. "I command you to tell me who you are!" she demanded vehemently.

"Who are you to command me?"

Hildegrinnel laughed. "I am Hildegrinnel of the Order of Six. Master of nature and healing, and I will demand and you will obey! Who are you?"

"The Order of Six? Of course. I will oblige you, Hildegrinnel. I am the King of the Nine Isles, once and true, and I will return and reclaim my kingdom."

"This is not your kingdom!" Hildegrinnel roared back. The shield had begun to fail as her strength waned. "Tell me your name!"

"You know my name, for you and your brethren are the ones who imprisoned me, and I will have my revenge!"

The column of fire became red as blood, its heat doubling, as it shredded through the last of Hildegrinnel's magical barrier and enveloped the assassin in its deadly luminance. The force of the evil magic threw Hildegrinnel, the captain and his men to the ground.

There was a scream and the column of fire vanished as quickly as it had formed. In the place where the assassin had been there was now a mound of ash and a plume of steam rising from within.

Hildegrinnel was helped to her feet by the captain of the city guard. "Who was that?" he asked her, sweat dripping from his brow and his legs trembling.

"I don't know, captain," she answered back, not knowing or understanding what the voice had meant when it said, 'you and your brethren are the ones who imprisoned me'. She had no memory of such an event. "Captain, would you be so kind as to fetch a coach to take me back to the palace? My strength had left me," she requested.

"At once, my lady."

4
A LIFE ALONE

ONE

The dragon was having that nightmare again. In truth it was more like a dream wrapped in a nightmare, and wrapped in a dream again. She went through that gauntlet in her mind most nights, and to her good fortune, she rarely remembered having them.

The events of the dream were always the same, she was soaring above the world, so high that the horizon curved slightly. The clouds around her were wispy and paper thin as she sailed in the air. Ahead of her she could see her family and the others like her. They were all traveling the great distance from Revelstoke to a land in the east, a trip they made every thirty years, but for what reason she couldn't remember.

The sun rose higher and higher, bathing the world in a warm glow, but suddenly black clouds swallowed the light beneath a crescendo of thunder that threatened to crack the sky in two. Heavy rain and violent winds buffeted her in an orchestra of air and water that stole her sight and rattled her being. Her wings trembled with great effort to stay aloft, but it was like the heavens were trying to force her from the sky. She cried out to her father and mother but they were no longer in front of her, or if they were she could not see them and the sounds of the storm drowned out her voice.

Lightning struck her, searing hot and flashing the most brilliant blue. The pain was searing and crippled her enough that she could not use her wings. It was then that she began to fall to earth, piercing the veil of the storm until she clearly saw the valley at the center of the ring of mountains, concealing it from the rest of the world.

She fell faster and faster and plunged into Edgewater Lake with a deafening splash and sank to the bottom as though she were a boulder. High above her she could see the surface of the lake. She began swimming toward the surface and when she broke through she was magically tumbling along the ground within the thick fields of wheat. Laying on her back she became aware of someone on her chest.

She looked down and saw a little girl in a yellow sundress napping on her, and in her arms was an odd, patchwork doll.

She knew the little girl as well as she knew herself. Her name was Arie. There was no mistaking that with her curly hair, like a fiery sunset, and full, cheeks beset with the cutest dimples. She couldn't have been more than eight or nine years old.

The dragon threw her arms around Arie and

hugged her tightly, as if she hadn't seen the child in ages. Tears of joy fell from her cobalt blue eyes. When Arie awoke she giggled, wriggled free and sprang away on two tiny feet.

"Come on, Kae! It's supper time! Let's get home!"

The dragon, whose true name was quite difficult say, but in the common tongue, was pronounced Kaezanneth, bounded after her like a lost puppy. The two of them skipped through the wheat field toward their home beneath a clear blue sky and the warm sun. Birds soared high above the vast fields, decorating the world with their sharp, chattering songs.

When they arrived at the house they found Arie's mother and father happily preparing supper and setting the table in front of their cobblestone farmhouse. An open hearth, made of fired clay, was cooking strips of deer meat and potatoes within the maw. Sitting on the weather worn table was a clay pitcher of homemade meadow-berry juice along with plates and utensils.

Arie plopped onto the edge of bench on one side as Kaezanneth sidled next to her on the ground. She was much too big to sit like everyone else, but that fact didn't bother her. She was with the family that had adopted her just a eight months ago, and being with them filled her with such elation that she was sure nothing happening right now was real.

Arie's parents sat across from her, then her older brother arrived from town and after exchanging pleasant smiles to each other, sat next to his sister. The food was passed, plates filled with herb roasted meat and salted potatoes, and mugs filled with berry juice. When everyone began to eat, the world grew dark as though the sun had just gone down.

Kaezanneth looked to the sky, confused and ashamed that she was in fear of something that was about to happen that she could never change. The sounds of struggled coughing made her look at her adopted family. They all had turned a shade of gray with dark bags under their eyes. Their faces were thin, and bodies even more so, then they fell to their knees and succumbed to a fate that already happened a long time ago.

Kaezanneth was horrified, her heart hammering with such force she thought it would burst from her chest. She cried out and rushed to Arie first, catching her before she could fall.

Arie looked up at the dragon, whom she regarded as a sister, and touched her muzzle. "Help, Kae! You can help us all, can't you?"

"I will help you! I'll go get Fendel! He'll know what to do!" Kaezanneth cried frantically and bolted away toward town to see the physician. When she reached the bridge into town she stumbled into a dead stop. Her jaw dropped at the sight of hundreds of bodies that lay on the cobblestone streets of the town. Most were dead, while others still suffered immeasurably with fits of coughing and enduring great pain in their chests. All of them had the same gray complexion as Arie and her family.

"What's happening to everyone!?" screamed Kaezanneth in a panic. She galloped to each person in turn, helplessly trying to render aid, but she had no medicine and knew nothing about alchemy to craft a cure. Her hope was slipping away as she raced through town in search of Fendel, but when she found him, he was already dead.

Kaezanneth spun and looked to each body that had fallen. All dead without a reason, and so suddenly that there was nothing the young dragon could do but watch them suffer and die.

Everyone, except for her.

Why wasn't she sick? Why wasn't she coughing and suffering from terrible pain like Arie and her family? Why?

Thunder rumbled as dark gray clouds blotted out the sky. Lightning flashed and twisted across the blackness of night as if the divines themselves were enraged with one another. Then the rain fell heavy upon the valley and began to wash the bodies away like paint being thinned with solvent.

Kaezanneth dashed through town and raced across the bridge back to Arie's house to find that no one was out front. The hearth was nothing more than a few broken clay bricks and the table reduced to a rotting husk. She spun to go toward the house but was confronted with four, large misshapen stones looming over her as if they were judging her. Low, muttering voices whispered to her, indistinguishable, but in a tone that sounded like they were scolding her, and the stones themselves began to lean unnaturally toward her as the rain fell and the sky growled.

She cowered from the stones like a frightened dog, feeling the weight of their meaning, and cried out, "I'm sorry! I'm so sorry! Please forgive me! Please!"

TWO

Kaezanneth jolted upright with a terrible start and slammed her head into the rafters of the tiny bedroom. It was barely large enough for her head and neck, but she managed to fit. One hundred year old dust showered on her head, and drifted into her nose causing her to sneeze violently, the force of which kicked up the dust once more and formed a thick, beige cloud. She quickly scooted out of the room while sneezing a few more times, and into the corridor her body occupied. It connected to the front room, but the rest of her length actually went out a large hole made in the wall of the house leading outside. She slept there every night, and it was enough to keep the rain off her during the spring rains and stave off the winds of winter that cut her like a million knives.

Wincing, she rubbed the spot that struck the ceiling, and checked to see if any of her short, rounded horns had been damaged. Luckily they were still intact. She then plucked a small, ragged doll stitched together oddly, and placed it atop a pile of old, aged blankets covering a broken and decaying wooden bed frame.

She yawned loudly then backed out of the house to face the day. A cool late-autumn breeze greeted her as she came out of the dilapidated house that was cobbled together with irregular stones whose mortar had dried up a long time ago. The roof was riddled with holes and the wooden tiles brittle with neglect from years unnumbered.

Kaezanneth stretched to her full length, nearly twenty feet from tail to nose, and was easily eight feet tall. For a dragon she was small, because she was very young, and it showed in more ways than one. Her head was crowned with a bony plate, that fanned outward slightly, and had four rounded, short horns that were swept backward. Her body was covered in scales on her backside, while her underbelly was soft like the skin of a human. The most striking characteristic she had was that her color changed from blue to teal to black depending on how light touched her.

When walking she tended to use all four of her limbs, but her front 'legs' acted much like arms, and the feet attached were more like three fingered hands than actual feet. Her most prominent feature was the impressive three-jointed wings that sprang from above both shoulders. A small claw, called a thumb, protruded from the third joint and allowed her to climb more effectively. Lastly her powerful tail, which was one third her length and tipped with three fins, lazily undulated as though it had a mind of its own. It had many uses, but was primarily used for flying and as a weapon.

Kaezanneth gauged the morning around her. The sun was barely climbing the east, beyond the ring of mountains, rising from behind a terrible wall of blackened clouds out over the sea. Sparks of blue popped from within the massive storm as it crawled away from the valley. She thought nothing more of the storm, as it was not in the valley, and chose not to think of whatever poor victim it may find. In fact she hoped there would be no victim at all.

She fanned her wings, to get her blood flowing, then trotted over to four large, oval-shaped stones sticking out of the ground thirty feet from the house. They were buried upright and had markings scratched into their surface.

Kaezanneth gently kissed each stone, her face saddened, before she turned quickly and bolted into the fields of tall, untended, withering wheat that blanketed much of the valley.

It was time to hunt.

THREE

Kaezanneth prowled among the wheat, carving her path in such a way that prevented her from disturbing the shafts too much, and kept as low as possible despite her large size. She didn't want to alert her breakfast, whatever it may be this morning. Her preference was yalat bird, because of its four wings and they tasted good, but she usually saved them for the end of the day. In the morning she generally ate one of two things, if she was lucky to get a chance at both, and they were field mice, and rabbits.

Field mice she did not like. They were too small, hard to catch, and it took a dozen to even satisfy the rumbling in her stomach, and when she cooked them with her fire breath, she almost always burned them.

Rabbits, on the other hand, were her favorite in the mornings, and like mice they were fast and very nimble, but were easier to catch because they were bigger than the mice. They were also easier to cook without burning them. It was rabbits that she wanted, but she would take whichever she found first.

Now, dragons have the most amazing sense of smell among all the creatures in the Nine Isles. So much so that they could track a scent through water, something that no dog or wolf could do, or detect a animal from more than a mile away and even identify it. When a dragon has a scent, there is no escaping from it.

Kaezanneth crept along and was nearly a mile from the house when she caught a scent of several rabbits. The scent from a rabbit, to a dragon, is sweet, but vanishes very quickly. She sniffed at the air for only a moment, then turned and followed the smell with the swiftness of an arrow in flight. When she was within a few feet she saw the tail of a brown rabbit as it dashed through the thick grass. She ran faster and bounded over the tops of the wheat in a graceful arc, looking down on her breakfast as it darted side to side.

Kaezanneth came down but the rabbit heard the dragon and doubled back just as she landed. She whirled back, digging her claws into the soft earth, then bolted after the small, furry critter. The chase was on!

Kaezanneth loved this part of the hunt. The exhilaration of pursuing a quick, agile and cunning prey such as a rabbit sent her heart racing and filled her with a small amount of joy. Of course, once the prey was caught, that joy would turn to a necessary act of survival.

The rabbit moved like a bolt of lightning, making tight turns at such odd angles that Kaezanneth had difficulty keeping up. Then, quite by surprise, it suddenly doubled back once more, and scampered under the dragon in the opposite direction.

Kaezanneth snapped at the rabbit as it passed, but missed. She lowered to head to look under her. From that point of view the ground and rabbit were upside down, and looked very funny to her. Without warning, one of her horns dug into the earth and catapulted Kaezanneth through the air where she tumbled along the ground. Chunks of dirt and wheat stalks flew in every direction as she destroyed the tall grass under her tumbling bulk. She laughed as the world spun around her, then recovered and continued the chase.

This is so much fun! She thought.

The rabbit darted west and broke through the wheat where an old dirt road separated the farm fields. It was racing for a large berry-bramble on the other side, that was most likely where its den was, and if she made it there, Kaezanneth would be unable to catch it. Or so the rabbit believed, if a rabbit believed in anything.

As the rabbit reached the middle of the road a shadow fell over it. Kaezanneth had leapt above the road, her wings wide and full, catching the morning sunlight. When she was positioned over her prey, she thrust those very same wings downward with as much strength as she could muster until the tips touched one another. A powerful gust of air struck knocked the rabbit into the earth, stunning it.

Kaezanneth landed, straddling her catch, and pinned it to the ground with both of her hands. The rabbit let loose a high pitched squeal in rapid succession, piercing the serene silence of the valley, and squirmed desperately against the dragon's iron grip. She could feel its heart thrumming as quickly as a hummingbird's wings.

The poor thing was absolutely terrified, and to Kaezanneth the only way to end such fear, was to make the kill quickly. She lowered her head and opened her mouth to bite but a new odor made her stop. To say it was a new odor is not entirely accurate, because the odor was more similar to the rabbit in her clutches than something totally new.

Kaezanneth lifted her head to trace the smell and noticed something in the bramble. Several pairs of eyes were watching her among the thicket of twisted and gnarled vines and clusters of berries. They were also skittering and scampering and hopping very excitedly.

Oh no, Kaezanneth thought, those eyes cannot be what I hope they are not.

She sniffed the air one more time, and felt her heart sinking in her chest. The eyes belonged to three baby rabbits, or more accurately, kittens.

Two were brown like the one she caught and the other was black.

After a moment of thought, Kaezanneth concluded that she had caught their mother. This changed the result of her hunt. She looked at the rabbit in her claws, then at the kittens peeking at her from across the road. She did this several more times, struggling to decide what to do.

Does she kill her catch, or set it free? She loved roasted rabbit, it was her absolute favorite, and this particular rabbit was slightly larger than the ones she usually caught.

Her mouth watered in anticipation as she shrugged off any thought of the kittens and lowered her jaw to finish her debate. The sounds of the kittens feet pattering around distracted her again and she sighed, then glimpsed over at the bramble. Three sets of tiny eyes, beset in fluffy faces, with pink noses that twitched, watched intently as their mother's life was being decided by a large, hungry dragon.

Kaezanncth sighed long.

Why are they watching me? Stop watching me! she thought incessantly and looked down at the mother rabbit struggling in her grip. The look of fear in the small animal's eyes tugged at her heartstrings.

Kaezanneth growled her disappointment as she set free her prize. The rabbit raced directly into the bramble and vanished.

I didn't want rabbit anyway, she thought. I'll go fishing instead!

FOUR

Edgewater Lake rippled under the autumn breeze, its water a pristine blue and surrounded by a sand covered shore much like the shorelines that are touched by the seas of the world. The lake was fresh near the top, and like seawater at the bottom, due in part to being fed from the Sea of Ellamar through submerged tunnels. Because of this, the lake supported both freshwater and saltwater fish.

Kaezanneth swooped low, just barely over the tops of the trees of a vast forest bordering the lake on the north side, and landed on the beach, trotting to a stop at the waters edge. She happily trotted along the edge of the lake before entering the water. It was a colder than she expected and made her reconsider fishing, but the hunger pangs in her belly forced her to press on. She drew a huge breath, dove into the water and darted away swiftly like she was a fish herself.

Almost immediately she caught the glint silver coming from a large group of silver-amberjack fish. Each was nearly the size of a man, and had gold along their sides in the shape of a chevron.

More importantly, silver-amberjack weren't

very fast in cold water, and the lake was considerably cool this morning. Kaezanneth darted toward them and the entire school zigzagged to try and throw her, but she didn't fall for it. She opened her mouth to spit a fireball but it exploded in her open maw, snuffed out by the water. The force of the collapsing air caused by her attempted attack created a shockwave that, like the rabbit from earlier, stunned several of the silver-amberjacks.

Kaezanneth swooped at, and snatched three of the fish, then using her wings, she whizzed upward and broke the surface of the lake. She flung open her wings once in the air and glided to the shore.

One and done! She thought proudly of her prowess as a fisherman.

She spit the large amberjacks onto the ground nearby and threw herself onto them, rolling until their scent covered her entire body. It was a practice that dragons did to establish ownership of a catch. Once she felt she was thoroughly painted in their smell, she snatched one up and threw it into the air. She then watched it hover over her mouth where she drew in a breath and let fly a focused plume of deadly hot fire from the pit of her stomach.

The flames made a roaring sound as it cooked the fish in mid-air a few feet above her waiting mouth. When a smoky scent filled her nostrils she extinguished the flames and allowed her freshly cooked meal to fall into her gullet. Her strong jaws and sharp teeth made short work of the smoked amberjack, and she swallowed it after only a few chomps. She did this two more times for the other amberjacks before returning to the water for a long drink.

Satisfied, Kaezanneth galloped into the forest toward town to perform a chore she always did after breakfast.

FIVE

Kaezanneth slowed to a steady trot as she exited the forest and followed the weed covered dirt road into the only town in the valley. It was also completely abandoned and in disrepair. The stone that made up most of the town's buildings was extremely weatherworn, and those structures that were made from wood were rotting under the cold winters and hot summers. Tall weeds sprouted along the ground against the walls and vines crept from within cracks in the walls on nearly every building. The roads in the village had once been cobblestone, but were now caked so much that it all was nothing more than dirt.

The silence of the town would make any stranger sad, and on some days it did that to her, but not today. This time she had forgotten the nightmare of last night and only happy memories floated to the top of her mind.

This town was a happy place once, long ago, and even though the folk that lived here at that time were now long gone and nothing but memories, those memories were like treasure to her. She marched through town and every dark shop or marred doorway only reminded her of a time when life flourished here.

Still, a day never went by that she didn't wish that none of these good people would've died so horribly, so painfully, and so young. Deep inside her, however, she felt responsible for being unable to help them, and she had a way of coping…

Each day, after breakfast, she would go to the church where the cemetery was, and clean the dirt and weeds from each of their gravestones. Then she would do the same to the graves she dug in the road around the church. When the cemetery had no more room, it was she that buried them in the road.

She hated having to do that, digging the graves, to see so many die that she cared for and having to lay them under the ground, but there was no one left to do so…at the end. To honor them, she kept their resting places tidy.

Today was no different. She spent the next three hours pulling weeds and blowing dirt from the stones until every one was to her liking. When that task was completed she made her way to the town's courtyard where a dried fountain sat in the middle of the road. West of the fountain was a short bridge that went over a narrow, quiet river. The old, dying buildings that encircled the courtyard were once shops and businesses where busting activity once took place, but now it was still and absent of life.

As Kaezanneth began to head toward the bridge she smelled a disgusting odor, and it was coming from her! She tucked her nose close to her unfurled wing and inhaled an awful stench. Fish!

She quickly jerked her nose away and gasped for air.

I need a bath, she thought.

Not wanting to waste any more time, she launched into the air and flew, just above the treetops and no higher. She headed northeast, with only one agenda on her mind, a bath, and the only place to do so was in the hot springs.

SIX

The hot springs were nearly twenty miles away and took five hours to walk, but for a flying dragon, the trip only took fifteen minutes. She made a pass over the wide expanse of pools and geysers to choose which she would use. In the morning sun the water in the pools was as green as jade stone, while others were bluish-gray. Fissures hissed and steam rose from the springs, inviting and enticing her to land and take a dip. Geysers nearby spewed towers of boiling hot water hundreds of feet into the air and soaked the ground, turning it to rings of warm mud.

Dragons hate cold, so much so they would rather have their wings removed than experience a winter snow. By the same token they equally love warmth, and have a tendency to make their homes near or inside volcanoes.

Kaezanneth, on the other hand, had no volcano to seek comfort from the winters, but she did have the hot springs. Every winter she spent the majority of her days here until it was time to sleep, then she went to her house and suffered the night with only a small fire to warm her. She would have it no other way no matter how uncomfortable she was.

Kaezanneth touched down near the mud rings with much delight. She pranced right into the mud until it was up to her belly, then buried herself to her neck with only her head and wings still exposed. The warm mud was like a thick, gooey blanket that filed in every crevice of her scales sending ripples of comfort throughout her body.

For a long time she lay in the mud, sometimes motionless, other times wriggling around, and twice she submerged her head. She buried her nose a few times and blew mud-bubbles, giggling like a small child when they popped. The geyser at the center of her pond erupted a dozen times while she bathed, and after that she finally dragged herself out and shook the mud loose like a wet, shaggy dog.

She spent the next hour lazily floating in one of the pools, then resting by the edge with her arms on the rim and her head tilted back, looking at the passing clouds. Large gib-jaxes, a kind of cricket the size of a small bird, occasionally ventured onto the rim and collected algae to take back to their nest. Kaezanneth plucked one as it hopped onto the edge, and flipped it into her mouth. It was crunchy and tasted like a peanut.

When more showed up she ate them, too. She did this for thirty more minutes before finally springing from the pool and again shaking herself dry. She surveyed the western sky to find the sun was getting close to the mountains.

It was time to go home and find supper. There was still three hours of daylight left, leaving plenty of time to hunt before she did her favorite thing for the evening, and that was stargaze.

She broke into a run, leapt with her wings spread and caught the warm air from the springs. It helped carry her into the air and once she was airborne she raced away. She kept low, only two dozen feet above the tall, grassy fields, and zipped past with such speed and silence that the small rodents on the ground never heard her approach. She banked southwest for the village, and home.

SEVEN

Kaezanneth landed gently in front of her home and started to go into the fields on the north side to hunt for supper, when a very familiar scent stole her attention. She hadn't had a visit from the owner of this smell for a few weeks, and she was beginning to worry.

A wave of enthusiasm, and a small amount of anger, washed over her. She whirled then rushed around the house and went into hole leading to her room. Immediately she noticed that the doll she slept with every night was missing from its spot on top of the old blankets.

Letting out a low growl that made her chest rumble, she backed out of the house and began tracking the smell. She knew exactly who had taken the doll. He had done it several times before to add to a nesting burrow, and each time he changed the location.

Normally, taking the doll would incite a rage in her the likes of which would frighten a dozen men, but when it was this particular individual, it was more of a game than a theft. She was also ten times bigger than him, and to fly into a mad attack against so small an opponent was a dishonor to her kind.

Once she knew the direction he had gone she broke into a hasty gallop into the fields. The scent trail led her southwest toward the western edge of the forest surrounding Edgewater Lake called Riverwood, nearly three miles from the house. Anticipation threatened to consume her as the smell got stronger and stronger. Then the trail stopped at the tree-line, but the odor was all around her. It crisscrossed, backtracked and wove through the trees and the field as if he had been gathering nesting material from the area.

The burrow had to be close. It had to be here.

Kaezanneth put her nose to the ground and followed every trail like a bloodhound tracking a fox. She went this way and that, scrutinizing one spot after another, spun three times at one point where he had obviously lingered, before picking up a new trail that followed the trees further south.

He must have found an empty burrow really far from me this time, she thought, relishing this hide and seek game more than the other times.

She hurried along the edge of the forest for a few hundred yards, then hugged the ground with her belly. The smell of her quarry was very strong now, and she knew that his burrow had to be very close. Listening intently, she thought she could hear tiny feet scratching at the earth. It had to be him cleaning the burrow, which meant the doll was most likely inside.

Normally she would find him before he could make it inside the burrow with her doll, but he had managed to do so this time. She would have to dig the burrow up, and she hated the idea of ruining his find. With winter coming, he needed someplace to hibernate soon.

Creeping along, she came to a small lump of earth and saw the hind-end of who took her doll as he was backing out of the entrance. He was cleaning out the burrow he had found by pushing out loose earth with his hind legs, then lifted his head. It was a raccoon! Not just any raccoon, but THE raccoon! The one that was always taking her doll.

His tiny eyes locked onto hers just a few feet away.

Kaezanneth flashed her teeth in what could have been a smile, but it only frightened the raccoon. When he tried to scurry into below ground, she raised onto her hind quarters and smashed her feet-hands into the mound and collapsed the entrance. She let out a grunting sound that was her way of laughing.

The move stunned the raccoon and he scampered through the tall grass with Kaezanneth at his heels.

Arie's doll! she exclaimed silently, and changed direction, racing back to the mound to search for it. When she found the entrance to the burrow, she dug into the dirt and found a tunnel, but it was only a few feet deep, and the doll wasn't there.

What, where is Arie's doll? she thought frantically. An emptiness tore its way into her chest and she felt like she couldn't get any air. Her breathing quickened pace as she frantically searched for the doll in the grass, and with each passing minute she felt worse and worse.

No, no, no! Where is it? Where is it? she repeated in her mind like a child who had lost their favorite toy.

She began pacing, her heart hammering hard in her chest while the emptiness in her stomach grew until it started to hurt. Tears filled her large, tapered eyes that resembled a cat's and, to add further embarrassment, she began to sob.

Maybe he dropped it on his way here, she thought, then rushed away to back track the trail.

She found nothing along the tree-line and continued northeast through the wheat field in desperation. Hope was slipping away, like sand in an hourglass pouring into the lower bulb, grain by grain. Each second tore a piece of her happiness away.

She should've hidden Arie's doll somewhere the raccoon couldn't find it.

Somewhere he couldn't reach, but raccoons are clever animals, and usually get what they want.

Just when she thought her doll was gone forever, she found another scent that she knew. It was another animal she recognized. One that didn't get along with the raccoon, and liked to steal from him. This animal was even a better thief, too.

Why she didn't notice the smell before, she didn't know.

Kaezanneth felt her hope renewed and she tracked the new scent as it led north. She must have run a thousand yards before she heard the sound of rustling grass, as if something was being forced through the shafts of withered wheat. Something too awkward to maneuver properly.

The closer she got to this sound, the stronger the scent became and then, the sound stopped. The reason was evident as the sound had gone into a small patch of trees at the edge of the fields.

The sun was low in the west when Kaezanneth penetrated the tiny forest. She immediately began sprinting among the trees, smelling each in her search of the thief, but for every one that did not reveal anything, her hope of finding her doll dwindled. The sound of claws scratching some distance away made her turn and rush headlong to a large oak with a wide trunk and branches that spanned twenty feet in every direction. She threw her feet-hands onto the trunk and stood on her hind legs. Clinging to the tree as it struggled to climb, while holding Arie's doll, was a ferrigrif. It was covered in brown and white feathers, had a muzzle and nose like a stoat, and a long, but small body. It had four stubby legs, each with four toes and sharp claws that made it an excellent climber. On its back were a pair of small, eagle-like wings that were only strong enough for short, quick bursts of flight, which was the reason it was dragging the doll instead of taking to the sky.

When the ferrigrif looked down at Kaezanneth it hissed at her, baring a mouth full of tiny sharp teeth, then it scurried up the tree with the doll in tow.

Oh no you don't, you little scamp! Kaezanneth thought angrily. She disliked the ferrigrif very much. It was a mean little creature, and killed without regard for compassion, even when it wasn't hungry. The mother rabbit she had released earlier, the ferrigrif would've killed it and the babies. One day she found her raccoon friend bloodied from a fight it had had with the ferrigrif, and there was no clear reason for it.

Kaezanneth dug her claws into the giant oak's trunk and chased the ferrigrif up the tree, snapping branches and raining loose leaves and broken twigs onto the ground below. She roared her displeasure with her powerful lungs and it shook the very air like thunder.

The ferrigrif, even slowed by the weight of the doll, was still quite nimble and expertly scampered up the tree and onto a thick branch. It then scurried along the length of that branch with Kaezanneth close behind. She forced her way through the thick foliage without regard for anything but reclaiming her doll…Arie's doll. Her eyes burned hot with rage as she clambered onto the branch and chased after her nemesis.

The ferrigrif bounded along like a squirrel to the end of the branch and leapt from it to a nearby tree, using its wings to glide the short distance. This tree was smaller than the great oak, but no less imposing, and just as quickly as the feathered thief landed, it had traversed to the other side of the tree and jumped again.

Kaezanneth decimated the surrounding twigs with her flailing arms and also leapt into the air, where she spread her wings and dove in pursuit. She watched as the ferrigrif effortlessly went from one tree to another much faster than she could chase it. If she kept trying to follow the ferrigrif on his terms, it would take much longer to catch him than she would like.

She slammed into the second tree the ferrigrif had jumped into, breaking a number of branches where she knocked him into a tangle of twigs. She was on him in a heartbeat, and had she not postured her dominance with a deafening, guttural roar that again made the world tremble, she would have retaken her doll. The ferrigrif, squawking and fluttering its wings with panic, suddenly spit a sickly, pea soup colored liquid into her face.

Kaezanneth's eyes instantly burned like the sting of a bee, and a horrible stench hovered in the air. She rubbed her eyes as tears streamed from them and snot oozed from her tortured nose. She swung her head away from the terrible little ferrigrif and gasped for air, allowing it time to claw its way through the foliage, where it again jumped to an even smaller tree.

Kaezanneth had finally had enough of this game. She cupped her hands over her mouth and vomited fire that scorched her own face, burning away the acrid bile from her enemy. Her face, now blackened, no longer suffered the effects of the attack, and she lunged upward through the canopy of the tree.

Once airborne, she unfurled her wings and seemed to hang in the air for a moment. Her expression became predatory as her eyes held a glint of fire around the edges, then narrowed as her nostrils flared. Her mouth was a thin, hard line and from within she made a grumbling noise that sounded like a hundred lions growling at once. Her chest ballooned as she drew breath, making her appear larger, then she thrust her neck and head toward the tree the ferrigrif had escaped to.

She opened her imposing maw, and from the back of her throat there was a reddish-orange glow that grew more and more intense until a torrent of fire flew outward. The heat scorched the air as it raced across the short distance to the tree, where it ignited the crown, turning it into a brilliant fireball. The night became like day under her power.

No sooner had she done this when she realized that the ferrigrif wasn't the only thing in the tree, so was her doll! She gasped with a heart full of sinking despair.

"NO!" she wailed out loud, her voice echoing for miles. Her world began to crumble, piece by piece, upon that realization. The doll was the last link to her past and the life she had with Arie and the people of the valley. Now it was most certainly burned to ash because of her anger with a creature that knew nothing of good or evil. It was simply an animal, doing what animals do, and now she was no better.

Dragons were supposed to be enlightened, more so than any creature in the world, and she had dishonored herself and her kin.

As she hovered in the air in the warm glow of her disaster, she saw in the light of that calamity, the ferrigrif as it emerged from the tree. It was still holding her doll as it flapped its tiny wings and flew into another tree.

Renewed again, and this night was ripe with renewals, she sailed after him and tore into the tree with the same determination as before. However, unlike the other oaks, this one was too small to endure, and the trunk swayed under her landing, then snapped with a loud pop, and collapsed into the earth with a ground shattering thud.

The ferrigrif was thrown clear where he rolled and bounced a dozen feet. In a flash he was on his feet and scurrying through the tall, withering wheat. The tree behind him exploded violently in a shower of splinters, leaves, and bark as a dark, very large undeterred winged Kaezanneth bounded into the air and came down upon her rival.

The ferrigrif fell onto his back, releasing the doll, and tried to claw Kaezanneth as she planted her feet into the earth very hard on either side of him. He growled and hissed defiantly when she pinned his wing with a powerful hand into the ground. She then raised the other hand and poised it over him, preparing to crush him to death.

The ferrigrif writhed and clawed at her, and even bit her scaly arm, but nothing he could do would harm her. She was the alpha hunter in this valley. There was nothing here that could do her any harm, ever, and she could do whatever she wanted.

And right now, she wanted to end the ferrigrif's life for what he had done to her raccoon friend, and for taking her doll.

Instead of killing him right away, she observed him trying to fight her off, even though there was no hope. Why she did this she wasn't sure.

The way it was violently attacking her right now only added to her decision to kill it, but then it did something she did not expect. The ferrigrif began to whimper and was no longer struggling.

Kaezanneth lowered her hand so she could look upon her fallen foe, and what she saw stayed her hand. The ferrigrif's expression was crestfallen and his eyes were no longer filled with the same coldness as when she first saw them.

She couldn't kill him anymore. Not now. Not for taking her doll and not for being what it was.

Kaezanneth sighed, then picked up her doll and again looked into the face of the little ferrigrif. "Not yours, Arie's! Now, go home," she told it, but it did not understand her, and never would. She lifted her hand and the ferrigrif raced into the darkness. Victorious, Kaezanneth flew toward home with her doll pressed tightly to her chest, excited about her adventure. She landed in the front of her house and hurried around to the rear.

"Arie! Arie, I'm back from my adventure! I got your doll back from that wicked little ferrigrif!" she exclaimed with great joy, but no one answered her. "Arie?", but Arie still did not reply, because she wasn't there.

Kaezanneth went into house and stuck her head into the bedroom that used to be Arie's, but it was where she slept now. To her extreme disappointment, Arie was not there. She backed out of the room and went around to the front of the house. It was dark and empty like it always was.

Then she remembered that Arie and her family had passed on long ago, as well as the townspeople. Her mood sank like a stone into water and her chest ached with immense sadness. She lumbered back the way she came and went to the burial stones behind the house. Her tail dragged the ground and her wings drooped at her sides. Tears filled her eyes as she went to the stone that was Aire's, where she curled up on the ground, gripping the doll close to her.

In her excitement of reclaiming the doll, she lost herself in the moment and forgot that she was alone in the valley. She had been for a long time, and did not know if she would ever see another person, human or otherwise, ever again.

She sobbed quietly at the foot of Arie's stone, her face wet, and whispered to herself, "I don't want to be alone anymore. I wish I had a friend again."

Just before she fell asleep, someone heard her plea, and had already sent someone, but he was going to be a little late…

5
THE MAELSTROM, THE ARGUMENT
AND THE FUNERAL

ONE

Luck was in favor of the Leonora Ander and her crew. On the morning of the third day they had turned to port and headed north toward the waters of the Iron Channel. The winds were at their back before the turn, but now it was hitting them broadside, and the result was a loss of speed. Even still the bow cut through the frigid waters faster than most other ships her size.

On the port side of the ship, miles away, was the Horn of Dameron, a peninsula of mountains topped year long with brilliant white snow. The stormy clouds behind it climbed ever higher in the sky, and rippled with lightning as it seemed to be racing to beat the Leonora Ander to the channel.

After six hours the sea became more rough as the maelstrom closed in, throwing huge walls of water across the bow of the ship and spilling over the deck. Within a few more hours the waves had become more and more violent until the ship rose and fell with the undulations like an out-of-control roller coaster.

The great sheets of heavy rain were next to punish the ship and her crew just before the winds arrived to tear her apart. The crew scrambled to keep the ropes tight that had been used to cinch the sails at one-quarter to prevent damage. Tired, drenched, and cold they fought on for their very lives. The deluge of nature was so loud that they had to scream to each other to communicate, but it was barely good enough.

Rikter fought with the wheel as he followed every order Captain Jones gave him. She was next to him, clinging to the mizzenmast with a sextant in one hand. She had been trying to find the stars to navigate by, but when the sky grew dark and the weather nasty, they became essentially blind. The Horn of Dameron had disappeared behind high chop and the blackness of nighttime.

Brice barked commands to the crew from the top of the steps to the quarterdeck, holding tightly to the rail as he relayed Captain Jones' words. The older man was exhausted and tiny crystals of ice clung to the fringes of his beard. "The storm has caught us, Captain!" he shouted.

Captain Jones snapped at him. "It caught us hours ago, Mr. Kinsdale!"

"We're lost!" Rikter cried.

"That we are!" Captain Jones agreed. "But we are not dead, Mr. Waycross! Keep a keen eye for the lighthouse on the Horn! We may yet be able to see it!"

Rikter didn't think it possible. The storm was preventing them from using the stars and the shoreline to navigate. For them to see the lighthouse on the Horn would be next to impossible.

"I doubt we'll see it, Captain!" called out Brice.

Captain Jones grimaced at his remark.

"Hold on! Hold on!" Rikter warned at the top of his lungs. Directly ahead of them was a wall of icy water the size of a mountain.

The ship climbed the surge then plunged a hundred feet down the backside of the wave. Spray kicked upward from the port and starboard sides of the bow like giant wings of white lace as it raced to the bottom. The bow plunged below the water then bobbed to the surface. The thunderous roar of the crashing water filled their ears and left them ringing. Crewmen and women were sent skittering across the deck like spilled marbles.

"Hold fast! Tie yourselves down!" Brice ordered.

The ship suddenly lurched forward with great speed, almost taking the feet from under Rikter, Brice, Captain Jones and the crew.

Captain Jones' eyes became wide with alarm. "Mr. Brice, what in the Divines was that?" she shouted.

"I don't know, Captain!" Brice yelled back. He looked to Rikter. "It felt like the currents are twisting!"

Rikter shrugged.

From beyond the darkness, and the storm itself, far over the port side of the ship, something bellowed like a million trumpets then grumbled as it faded. The sound ricocheted off the waves and clouds, cutting through the air with such force that it made their chests tremble. It filled each of the crew with a dread not unlike a child's fear of the dark.

The sound erupted again in the blackness. It was louder and longer than the first and was followed by a crash like the crumbling of a mountain.

"Could it be thunder?" Rikter asked, gripping the wheel so tightly his fingers grew numb.

The storm around them continued to attack the ship, but none aboard were as concerned with it as before. They all scanned the blackened sky in the direction of the strange noise, and none knew what it was. No storm anywhere had ever produced such a sound, and no creature that roamed the land had ever been heard making a sound like it, either.

"It's the Divine of the sea come to destroy us!" cried one of the crewmen.

"Hold your tongue, crewman!" Brice sneered.

The mysterious sound boomed again as

though it was upon them this time. Where it came from was shrouded in swirling clouds and rain so thick the lightning was nearly snuffed out. Only glimpses of blue peeking from cracks in the air told them where the heart of the storm was.

"Mr. Waycross, turn us to starboard!" Captain Jones ordered. The pit of her stomach was in knots with fear. She hoped that by turning starboard, they would head into The Grand Eastern Sea and escape the Great Storm, of which she was certain was what they had failed to avoid.

"Aye, Captain!" Rikter shouted and he turned the wheel furiously to the right. The bow felt like it had swung where it was supposed to, but within the tempest there was no way to be sure if it had done so.

"I cannot tell if we turned!" Rikter called out. His heart threatened to beat its way from his chest.

Brice looked to the aft of the ship. The eye-wall of the Great Storm flashed before his eyes in the flutter of a bolt of lightning. There was something behind the thick veil of the calamity, casting a shadow onto the air and water. It writhed, rising high above the surface of the sea, then fell hard and vanished behind a tall wave chasing the ship. He squinted against the rain and wind, straining to see if the shadow would appear again.

"There's something in the eye of the storm!" he called out.

Captain Jones looked at Brice, then turned to

see what he was looking at. "Impossible! Nothing could survive in there!"

"I'm telling you Captain, there's something in that storm!" he shouted.

A flash of lightning threw a shadow onto the eye-wall. It was fifty stories tall and as thick as ten redwood trees. The shadow wriggled in the air, then was followed by another, and another, then another.

Whatever they were, there was four of them now.

The four shadows crashed downward and the sea trembled as a tremendous serpent like creature, whose size was nearly equal to a mountain, sprang through the veil and plunged below the water. It had a tremendous maw as wide as a valley and inside were thousands of sharp, white teeth. A great swell rippled through the sea where it had dove and shoved the Leonora Ander sideways.

"By the Divines!" screamed Brice. He rushed to Captain Jones' side. "It's a sea serpent, Captain!"

The crew began to cry out upon seeing the monstrosity, panic seizing each person by their heart and wringing it without mercy. They rushed to unfurl the sails, not waiting to be ordered to do so. A mistake they would soon learn.

Captain Jones was frozen with panic at the behemoth she had beheld. Never in her life had she ever seen such a large beast, nor had she ever heard tales of such a thing. She suddenly felt very small on her ship.

"Is that thing the cause of the Great Storm?" Rikter asked, his voice shrill.

"Does it matter boy?" Brice stammered. He noticed the crew on deck, rushing up the shrouds, and untying the ropes and sails. They were frightened and their only thought was to catch the wind and flee, but in the twisting wind it would only rip the sails apart. He ran to the rail at the wheel and shouted below.

"No! Stop!"

Behind the Leonora Ander the enormous serpent again leapt from below. It twisted in the air and veered away from the ship, plunging back into the water. The hide of the great beast was covered with overlapping, silvery-green scales, each the size of a mud-brick house. Trailing behind the monster were four thick, muscular tentacles whose ends were spade shaped, like the tail of a fish. The whole of the creature somehow vanished into the maelstrom it was obviously responsible for creating.

The Leonora Ander veered toward the heart of the storm without warning, pulled by the fast moving sea as helpless as a leaf in the wind. The sails began to tear from their riggings, and the ropes that had held them in place whipped and thrashed the deck and crew, who tried desperately to wrangle them. Then a crewwoman looked toward the blackened sky and heard a sound like wood being twisted.

"Look!" she shrieked, pointing into the darkness.

Brice glanced where she was pointing and froze in astonishment.

The mangled hull of a sailing sloop hung in the air as it raced across the sky and plunged into the sea ahead of the Leonora Ander's bow. The shockwave knocked everyone off their feet and grabbing for anything to keep from going overboard.

"What was that?" Captain Jones demanded as she struggled to her feet.

"A ship! It was riding the wind behind that foul beast!" Brice shouted.

"What are we to do, Captain?" Rikter yelled to her as he picked himself up and fought to steer the ship.

Captain Jones didn't have an answer for her third-officer.

They all looked up as the bow broke through the thick wall of swirling clouds and water. Once on the other side of the barrier the rain stopped falling and the winds died down. Above them the sky was clear and alight with brilliant stars. It was the most serene sky they had ever witnessed, until the ship listed to the port side and showed them the true horror of the Great Storm.

Stretched for miles across, the sea was whirling in a great circle surrounded by the impossibly high wall of rushing air and torrents of rain. The center of the enormity fell hundreds of feet below the level of the sea whose bottom was no longer wet. Thousands of any manner of sea-life lay on the seabed, flopping helplessly, along with the wreckage of a hundred ships. Caught in the walls of the whirlpool were other sailing vessels long forgotten. Their wooden skeletons rotting or encrusted with barnacles as they rode the untamable wake of the large four-tailed serpent.

No one on the Leonora Ander had the courage, or the will to speak, as the ship careened over the edge of the event horizon into the whirlpool. She was now the newest member of the Great Storm's victims as the crew screamed in sheer terror.

Rikter clung tightly to the helm and strained to move the wheel, but it was impossibly stuck. "The helm will not respond!"

Captain Jones thought a moment and managed to utter. "The currents! They're too strong for the rudder!"

The ship continued to plunge then struck a passing wreck. The blow was enough to push the Leonora Ander into the current like the other trapped ships.

Rikter lost his grip on the wheel when they

collided and he slid into the port side rail. He wrapped his arms around it like a vise.

Captain Jones breathed a sigh of relief to see Rikter had not gone overboard. She took the helm and struggled to turn it. "Brice, help me turn the ship!"

Brice immediately ran to her and pulled on the wheel but still it refused to budge.

The serpent of The Great Storm blared its call, splitting the air, and all eyes turned. The beast was on the opposite side of the whirlpool jumping from the water like it had done before. Hanging from its wide mouth of teeth was a gray whale a hundred feet long. A slithery tongue slid out of the monster's mouth and wrapped around the bulk of the whale, then pulled it into its gullet in a single swallow.

"It's eating whales?" Rikter sputtered with disbelief.

"Better them than us, mister!" shouted Captain Jones.

The serpent delved back into the sea as quickly as it had appeared before the Leonora Ander shuddered from the impact of another wrecked ship. The two ship's main masts became entangled and the stress from the wreck pulling away snapped the Leonora Ander's main mast in two. It crashed to the deck nearly killing several crewmen.

Rikter rushed down to the main deck to help

the crew while Captain Jones and Brice fought futilely to wrest the wheel free.

A rope and tackle whooshed overhead from the lower portion of the main mast just a few feet above Rikter's head. It was spiraling around the broken beam, and before Brice could yell a warning it struck Rikter on its next pass in his back. It sent the young man tumbling across the deck. His foot found its way through a loop of tangled rope and cinched tightly around his ankle. As luck would have it the port rail halted his momentum.

Winded, he coughed as air was trying to fill his lungs. He lifted himself to his hands and knees very slowly. The world around him seemed to quiet down and he felt very dizzy.

"Rikter, are you okay, my boy?" Brice called out.

Rikter nodded, then when he tried to stand he felt the rope on his ankle. He reached to remove it then a crewman shouted.

"The cannon is loose! Look out!"

Rikter turned his head to watch the port cannon slide in his direction. He rolled to the side as it raced by and broke through the port side rail as easily as an axe through a melon. A single rope snaked behind the iron weapon as it succumbed to the sea.

"Rikter, your leg! The rope!" shouted Captain Jones who had run to the quarterdeck rail when the boy had fallen.

Rikter glanced at his leg, and the rope looped around his ankle. He traced the rope to where it went and his blood ran colder than ice.

It was attached to the cannon!

He struggled to free his foot, but it was too late. The weight of the sinking cannon snatched him and he was pulled toward the edge of the ship. Brice suddenly was upon him, landing on the deck on his belly, and grabbed one of Rikter's hands with both of his. Both men were pulled across the deck, but the older man folded his legs beneath him and caught the gunwale with his heels.

The movement had been arrested.

"Quickly boy! The knife I gave you! Cut your leg free!" Brice pleaded behind clenched teeth. The weight of the cannon was too much for him, and he did not know how long he could hold on. Two crewmen came to Brice's aid and each wrapped their arms around the old man's girth.

Rikter reached under his tunic for the knife and tried to reach his leg, but he couldn't. The cannon was far too heavy for him to lift his leg to make the cut.

"I can't reach, Brice! It's too heavy! It's going to tear my leg off!" Rikter looked up at his friend with sadness in his eyes. "You have to let me go!"

"No, boy! Never! I'm not letting go!" Brice cried out.

The serpent's wail rumbled behind the Leonora Ander as the behemoth exploded from the sea and smashed back into the water. It was so close to the ship they could smell the odious stench coming off it. It passed under Rikter like a dark shadow and swallowed, quite by accident, the cannon that he was attached to. He had time enough to glance at the monster and then back at Brice.

"That's not good!" Rikter shouted just before he was violently ripped from Brice's grasp and disappeared into the cold sea.

TWO

"You nearly killed him, sister!" the Divine of Wisdom, wearing the white cloak, exclaimed. She turned her glare to her sister in purple, the Divine of Chance.

"I did what was necessary. The boy needed to be off that ship," Chance said.

"Yes I agree, but did you have to make use of the Worm of Yeningregger?" Wisdom asked.

"I applaud her work. The boy is indeed off the ship and on his way to the valley of Dayle," the sister in the black cloak said. Her divinity was that of Courage. "Sister Fate, does the boy arrive in the valley of Dayle unharmed."

The Divine of Fate lowered the hood of her

blue cloak and went to the crystal ball of ice on the table. In it she gazed peacefully. "He does, Sister Courage, but he will not awaken."

"Oh dear," gasped Wisdom.

"Is he dead?" Courage asked, shooting Chance a cold sneer.

"He is not dead!" snapped Chance, feeling her pride had been tarnished by the oldest sister. "And I take offense that you would ask if the boy is dead after I told you he will be unharmed!"

Courage sneered at Chance again. "I was not asking you! I was asking Wisdom!"

"I must look first," Wisdom sputtered, nervously going to the table. She disliked the way her sisters argued at times. "I don't think he is dead."

"Do you believe me now?" Chance spat.

"Then why does he not awaken?" Courage hissed.

They both turned to Wisdom who had slipped away from them and was by the window, feigning interest in the vast forest around their home.

"Well, Wisdom? Can you not tell us why he will not awaken?" Courage asked.

"I do not know. There is s shroud around him that I cannot penetrate," she told her.

"What do you mean by shroud?" Fate asked.

"It is like someone has thrown oil into my eyes when I try to see his spirit. I've never seen anything like it," Wisdom said. "But he is not dead."

Courage sighed with great relief, then turned to Fate. "And you see him later, when he has the throne?"

"I have," Fate said firmly.

"Then he must awaken eventually," Chance said.

"Yes," Fate answered.

"We have not failed," Courage declared. "There is still hope."

THREE

It had been four days since the Lord of Ellamar Greggory Baylen was poisoned and died in Lady Samarra's arms, and in that time a grand funeral to lay him to rest took place. Thousands of the citizens of Skyvale lined the cobblestone streets along the route to the Tomb of Lord Regents near Graymarch Fortress. The banner of House Baylen flew at each procession checkpoint, as hundreds of knights on horseback escorted the Black Coach on its journey. Eight black stallions pulled the twelve foot wagon, lavishly crafted with etchings of previous Lord Regents and writings of their deeds in life. Lord Greggory's would not be carved until he was laid to rest.

Royal Emissaries from all over Ellamar

flocked to the city and followed behind on foot, carrying the banners of their lineage, dressed in robes of purple and crimson. At the head of the long line of mourners was a lone chariot made of silver and bronze being pulled by three of the largest white horses in Ellamar. Lady Samarra and her son, Bremmen Baylen the Lord Knight of the Gray Knights, rode in this beautifully crafted chariot that was only used for such funerals.

Lady Samarra's cheeks were wet with tears but her eyes were angry amid the grief. Bremmen, on the other hand, was more stoic, but it did not mean he was without heart. He loved his father very much, and knew he had to be strong for his mother's sake.

Bringing up the rear of the long procession, riding a large pony named Strawberry, was Hildegrinnel. Her face was forlorn with the burden of the failure to protect Lord Greggory. Upon her return to the palace that dreadful day, she told Lady Samarra of the encounter at the docks, and the fire that fell from the sky and killed her husband's assassin. She detailed the conversation with the voice in the sky that made the claim of returning to retake the Nine Isles. She even told the Widow of Ellamar that the voice in the sky placed blame on Hildegrinnel and her colleagues for its imprisonment.

When Lady Samarra asked what they could do to stop the voice in the sky from returning,

Hildegrinnel only said, "We must go to the Athenaeum of the Ancients, but what to look for, I do not know, my lady."

In the presence of the mass of weeping onlookers, loyal citizens and saddened visitors, there was a nearly dead silence that permeated the city. Even the sky appeared to have been affected by Lord Greggory's untimely death, for sunlight had not touched the region through the thick, gray clouds.

The procession arrived at the tomb in the early evening and the Gray Knights dismounted, then marched to the rear of the Black Coach, and removed the royal casket. Made entirely of Inilthiandere Oak and trimmed with lapis and gold, Lord Greggory's casket was quite heavy in their arms.

The knights then carried the body of their lord, with Lady Samarra and Lord Knight Bremmen following, through the marble and granite entrance to the Tomb of Lord Regents. He was laid to rest deep under the small, but intricately decorated structure.

The tunnels and rooms below the entrance were kept very clean. The floors were polished diorite, a gray colored rock, and alcoves in the walls had statues of past kings frozen in poses of stoic grandeur. Torches at each statue lit the way to where they would inter Lord Greggory next to his father and mother.

The next morning the emissaries departed and the citizens of Skyvale awoke to the world without their beloved Lord Regent. To them, this new day, even with the sun peering over the eastern horizon under a cloudless sky, was not enough to hold back the sadness in their hearts.

Hildegrinnel found Lady Samarra at her table in the terrace where she would have breakfast with Lord Greggory.

Today he was not there, and never would be again. She was wrapped in her husband's fur robe and on the table lay his sword, Knaythrandire, the elvish word for 'peacekeeper'. The sunlight shining on her from the open terrace did nothing to warm her. She hadn't eaten since the day before the funeral and sleep eluded her empty bed. A redness painted the whites her eyes and her cheeks were wet with tears.

The witch quietly went to her side. "You sent for me, my lady?"

Lady Samarra wiped her swollen cheeks before saying, "Yes, Hildegrinnel. Thank you."

"My lady, I-"

"We need to discuss the Athenaeum you mentioned before," Lady Samarra said, unintentionally interrupting her.

"Yes, my lady, I thought as much. Tell me what you know of it."

"I know nothing of it," Lady Samarra said.

"Ah. First let me tell you, the Athenaeum is

a library," Hildegrinnel said.

Lady Samarra looked at Hildegrinnel, head tilted slightly in thought. "Library?"

"Yes, my lady, but not just any library. It is the oldest library in all the isles," Hildegrinnel began. "I cannot tell you how old, because my memory is not what it once was, nor can I tell you how it came to be, for no one can answer such a question. Not even I."

"Because you cannot remember?" Lady Samarra surmised.

Hildegrinnel nodded, ashamed. "I can tell you however, that we need to go there to find the name of the true king of the Nine Isles, and to learn if the voice was telling the truth when he claimed that I and my brethren imprisoned it."

Lady Samarra nodded her understanding. "When will you leave?"

"Very soon," Hildegrinnel said.

"I wish to go with you," Lady Samarra told her. It did not sound like a good idea to the witch, whose dumbfounded gaze grimaced back at her.

"Do you think that is wise, my lady?" Hildegrinnel asked.

"Honestly, I do not, but I want to go. I need to know who wanted Greggory dead and why."

Hildegrinnel understood Lady Samarra's need to seek out her husband's true assassin, and it was fueled by grief and an urge for vengeance, she was sure. Even though the witch did not believe in revenge, she had sworn service to the lord and lady of Ellamar for as long as she could remember.

"My lady, you have suffered a great injustice, but I sense that your desire to know who sent the assassin is just a means to exact revenge," Hildegrinnel said, sympathetically.

Lady Samarra's expression hardened. "And?" she asked.

"And, it is not revenge you need, my lady, it is justice."

"No, Hildegrinnel, I do not need justice! The people of Ellamar need justice, and deserve it! Their benefactor is gone and it is up to my son to lead them like his father! I want revenge because I deserve it! My husband has been taken from me, by a thief that would use guile to kill rather than a sword and open battle! There was no honor in my husband's death!" Lady Samarra hissed as she felt her heart breaking again.

Hildegrinnel stared back at her intently with sympathetic eyes.

"You do understand, don't you?" Lady Samarra asked. There was a gleam in her eyes that pleaded for acceptance.

Hildegrinnel nodded. "Yes, my lady, I do."

Lady Samarra nodded and for the first time in days her sadness began to turn into lethal determination.

"The journey will take five days, my lady.

Preparations need to be made immediately. I do not know how much time we have till this 'true king' returns," Hildegrinnel declared.

"Rafferty," Lady Samarra called for the steward standing just outside the room. He strode in and went to her side.

"Yes, my lady?"

"Summon Bremmen. Hildegrinnel and I need him here right away."

"At once, my lady," Rafferty said and hurried out of the room.

"What do we need to do, Hildegrinnel? Who do we need to make this journey?" Lady Samarra asked.

Hildegrinnel nodded. "The Gray Knights and a word with my brother, Grimmholder."

6
FROM THE BRINK...

The sand felt good on her feet. It was warm and tickled her toes as she walked gingerly to the young man lying on the beach. To her he appeared dead as gentle waves of lukewarm lakewater lapped his motionless body and still he did not stir. His clothes were tattered and face scratched with traces of drying blood winding down the curve of his cheek. His feet were bare, most likely his boots had been ripped free during the terrible storm, and were obviously lost to the sea.

The woman was wearing a flowing white robe beneath a brown cloak that dragged the ground behind her. She was tall and had long, curly, mahogany hair that fell to her ankles. A smile was stretched wide across her face and made her full cheeks stand out in the warm sunlight.

It had been a while since she had been to the Mortal World. It was a place that was far below where she was from.

The view from her apartment in the Divine Palace afforded her a splendid sight of the beautiful and colorful world.

However, she did not descend from the upper world to be a tourist. She had come to see to the boy, Rikter Waycross, who had been lost to the sea two days earlier. The light from his spirit had dimmed enough to alarm her, forcing an intervention. He hadn't moved in nearly a day and from where she lived, she could feel his life ebbing away.

But he was not dead yet.

As she knelt beside him she could feel eyes watching from far away, beyond the mountains and valleys and across the Southern Horn Sea north of Ellamar. She looked to the north and smiled at the unseen watchers.

"Sisters," she said and a voice traveled back to her on the winds.

"Aembrescolathia. Why do you venture where you are not needed?" The wind whispered back in a voice she knew.

"Angellevere. What are you and your sisters up to?" Aembrescolathia demanded serenely.

"That is our business and ours alone. Know this, it is for the good of all," The voice belonging to the Divine of courage, Angellevere, said.

"If that be your agenda, then why does this boy balance on the tip of life and death?" Aembrescolathia retorted.

"It was an accident!" snapped a different voice, belonging to the Divine of Chance, Gwendelor.

"Shut up, Gwendelor, I am speaking for us!" bickered Angellevere to her sister.

"And you are not doing as well as you

would like, are you?" chided Gwendelor.

"The both of you are too old to behave like children," Aembrescolathia said. "Why do you stall me?"

"We do not wish you to interfere," Angellevere told her.

"We must let her. It is the only way," said a third voice. This one belonged to Fate, Amandonia.

There was a brief moment of silence on the air before Aembrescolathia again spoke.

"If there are no more objections, I will take my leave from you now," she turned back to Rikter laying motionless in the sand, and leaned close to his ear. "You are not going to leave this world, young Rikter Waycross of Ironshire, son of Elizabeth." With a wave of her hand he rolled onto his back and his mouth fell open. "I breathe the air of life into you so that you may not cross over, and return to the living world." She pursed her lips and blew a wisp of air that whirled into his mouth.

Rikter woke up rather suddenly…

THE LOST VALLEY OF DAYLE
AND A DRAGON

ONE

Rikter twitched, then shot upright. Seawater spewed from his lungs in a violent cough. His eyes were as wide as the moon as his memory of the storm and the great beast dragging him under the water flashed through his mind. Then everything went black for what felt like years before he heard a woman's voice talking to him. She had said his name, and his mother's, or was it just a waking dream? A quick look around told him he was alone on the shore of a lake he had never seen before.

His whole body ached when he tried to stand, so he remained sitting and took in his surroundings.

The sun was slowly climbing the sky beyond the jagged mountains in the east. He stared at the peaks of stone so tall it seemed like they were taller than the sky itself and wondered what their names were, if they had names. He then twisted around to follow how far they stretched, and to his surprise the range of ridiculously high and imposing rock encircled where he was. Across the lake before him, several miles away, an imposing wall of ageless rock rose from the water and into the sky.

Rikter brushed sand from his hair and damp, ripped tunic and face, then winced when he rubbed a sore gash running from his brow to his jaw. He looked at his hand and was relieved to find there wasn't blood. He slowly climbed to his feet and surveyed what was around him.

He was on a beach that lined the northern, eastern and western sides of a lake that, as far as he could tell, smelled like seawater. Beyond the yellow sand of the shore was an immense line of tall trees, whose leaves had only begun to turn gold and brown, that went west and east as far as he could see. The ground around the forest floor was overgrown with a collage of thick, leafy foliage. Birds chirped and sang throughout the breadth of the forest like a thousand voices in a choir.

A fierce pounding sensation in Rikter's head made it difficult for him to be grateful for being alive and somewhere warm. Still he continued to take in his surroundings, and had he just plopped back onto his rear he would've missed the humble, weathered shack with the thatched roof near the forest.

Rikter made his way to the shack. "Hello!" he called out. "Is anyone here? My name is Rikter Waycross!" There was no reply from within and the closer he got, the more obvious it was that it was deserted, and had been for some time. He would have preferred there to be someone living in it that could tell him where he was. Regardless of his hopes, it was at least a roof to sleep under until he could find a town or people nearby, if there was any.

His stomach grumbled a complaint about being empty, but what could he do? He had only just arrived, as far as he knew, and hadn't even thought of or was even worried about food at the moment.

He stepped onto the rotting boards that were once a porch to the shack, and noticed his bare feet. He silently complained that his boots were gone.

Probably swept off my feet when I was being carted around by the sea serpent, he thought. Stupid animal!

He then suddenly thought of Brice, the Captain and the crew. Had they survived? If they did, did they think him dead? What else could they deduce after watching him plunge into the water with that sea monster?

His heart stammered for what felt like an eternity. He missed his friend and Captain Jones, and he hoped they were alive and well somewhere.

"Well," he said to himself. "I guess I'm alone here, wherever here is."

He opened the aging door to the shack and it fell off of the rusty hinges, kicking up dust. When it settled he went inside. It had an earthy smell that choked his lungs and he coughed. Sunlight peppered through holes in the roof revealing the interior. Against the furthest wall was an old bed frame and scraps of cloth that was once a mattress covering. A table and chair, both coated in a layer of sand, was in the middle of the small room, and in another corner was a cast iron cooking pot, rusted from years of neglect. Under the pot was a fire pit made from carved stone that was filled with ash. A four foot tall cupboard near the door was wide open and leaning in it was a pair of fishing poles made of Ulak, a wood that never ages or rots.

Rikter sighed and looked around again in case he missed anything. He did not miss anything. What he saw in the shack was what there was. "Well, it's like the storeroom back in Ironshire," he joked to himself. "Almost like home."

His stomach protested again. "Ok," he said and grabbed one of the fishing poles. He looked it over carefully. There wasn't any twine to cast attached to it. He sighed again as a complaint, then went outside.

There was plenty of day left, and even though he wanted to strike out and find civilization, he was also hungry. And the first rule of survival is to find food.

To fix the rod he first needed something to make twine with. He looked to the trees and went toward the forest. At the edge he noticed an overgrown footpath and he followed it a short ways until he found a green stalk of bamboo. Ahead of him all he could see was the unending thicket of the forest.

He wondered how large the forest was then turned his attention back to the bamboo stalk.

"Perfect. If I strip the stalk I could make twine," he again said to himself, then he smirked. "Who the heck am I talking to?"

He tore the thin stalk from the ground. It was easy since the entire plant was only a few feet tall, and dragged it back along the path. As he emerged from the forest the bamboo hung on something in the overgrowth.

Rikter looked back and tugged it free to discover that an old, rotting sign was clinging to the end. "Hmm," he hummed and turned the plank over.

Written on it in thick black letters were the words, "Village of Springwater" and an arrow pointing towards the heart of the woods.

"That makes things easier," he said cheerfully, and before he could drop the bamboo and the rod to head where the sign pointed, something near him, hidden in the dense growth, disturbed the foliage. He jumped with fright then froze.

Rikter's eyes darted as he tracked the sound moving within the thick vegetation. Then as quickly as the rustling noise had begun, it ceased.

If it had been a predator the birds would have stopped singing, but the forest was still filled with their call. Whatever was scurrying behind the leafy foliage had either fled, or was just as frightened as him and became as still as a statue. He turned and went straight to the shack to repair the rod.

Rikter had decided that he would rather eat first then find the village called Springwater. There was no way to know how far the village was from the lake and he wanted his strength restored before the journey. Besides, he thought, if whatever was skulking in the forest was a predator, he would at least be its dinner with a full belly first.

TWO

Kaezanneth crept slowly through the bushes and leafy plants at the edge of the forest, careful not to disturb what she had spotted on the shore. She watched intently the man-boy while he lay, unmoving, on the shore of Edgewater Lake. He couldn't have been there very long. She had just been at the lake two days ago to fish and he was not there. Sometimes creatures would find the lake from the outside world by means of an underwater tunnel. The fast moving currents drew in seawater from the other side of the mountains, and kept the lake supplied with fish.

She knew this because she had tried to use the tunnels to leave the valley but was too large to fit through. He was also smaller than her, so he must have come in that way, and it was a long tunnel so he must have drown. There-fore he had to be dead, she thought.

The scales on her back rippled along her spine with a soft clicking sound when, without warning, a second human took shape near the man-boy.

Where had this human come from? And it was a female! The female-human was very tall and had long, dark hair and went to the dead man-boy.

Kaezanneth's cat-like eyes narrowed, focusing on the female-human wearing the long brown robe, as she lowered herself near the man-boy. Then the female-human looked away to the north, and spoke to the wind.

What kind of female-human talks to the wind? she thought curiously. Is her mind gone?

She watched the female-human talk to the air for what felt like too long for her to be watching a female-human talk to the air. Then the female-human knelt to the man-boy, and he moved onto his back without the female-human touching him.

Kaezanneth cocked her head to one side as she tried to understand how the female-human moved the man-boy in such a way.

Next the female-human whispered and the air from her lips twisted and fell into the man-boy's mouth.

Then the man-boy awoke with a jerk and the female-human was gone like she had dissolved with the early autumn wind.

The disappearing female-human angered her with such deception. Where did the female-human go and what right did the female-human have to trespass in her valley without permission? Kaezanneth did not harbor any contempt for the man-boy because he had been dead, but now she was unsure of him.

She crouched lower in the thick ferns and palm leaves of the forest edge and cinched her wings closer to her back. She did not want him to spot her hiding, watching him. She was not afraid of the man-boy, but she used to hear Arie's mother tell tales about men beyond the mountains. There the men were cruel, and not just to those they did not know. They were cruel to everyone, and if this man-boy was from beyond the mountains, then he may be like them.

The man-boy tried to stand, then plopped back into the sand on his butt. This made her snicker and it disturbed the birds in the trees who began to chirp with excitement.

He was sure to hear the commotion, Kaezanneth thought.

She watched quietly as he sat there for a while before he tried to stand again. This time he managed to keep on his feet and he wandered away from her along the shore toward the fishing shack. She crawled on her belly through the undergrowth until she was ten feet from the overgrown path. Every time she saw the path the memories of Arie skipping along it to go swimming in the lake would creep back into her thoughts. She shook her head as though it could jostle the memory out of her ear and focused on the man-boy.

He had gone inside the fishing shack and the door was loose from the hinges and laying on the ground.

Did he tear the door loose? she surmised. Is he violent? He looked too stringy to have the strength to yank the door free.

After a few minutes the man-boy emerged from the shack holding a long rod that she knew to be used to catch fish. Kaezanneth expected him to go to the water but instead he went to the edge of the forest toward where she was hiding.

Slowly she inched backward but the end of a wing hooked a fern and she had to stop to keep from being heard by the man-boy. Her eyes narrowed and her heart hammered as she prepared to pounce on him if he found her. Luckily he turned onto the path and moved away.

She turned and ducked beneath an oddly

curved tree trunk, and circled wide around him where the forest floor had less growth. Through the thicket of the woods she caught glimpses of the man-boy as he slowly treaded the path. He appeared to be looking for something specific, but what that could be she did not know. He was also speaking to himself.

What a goober he is! Kaezanneth thought. He talks to no one!

Then she watched as he wrested a stalk of young bamboo from the ground. Not far from there he bent down and picked up an old plank of wood that was covered by vines and leaves. He turned it over in his hands and she was sure he had read the words there.

She moved closer to him and when she attempted to crawl under a large bush, one of her slender horns on her head became entangled and rustled the branches. She cringed as she saw the man-boy look in her direction, unmoving.

Her heart stopped beating and she held her breath.

The man-boy's head followed the noise to where she was hiding, and she was almost certain he saw her. When she noticed that his eyes were wriggling in his head she knew he could not find her.

After a moment he seemed to lose interest and turned away from her. She watched him walk back in the direction of the shack. When he was far enough away she untangled her horn and leapt onto the path. For her size she was incredibly nimble, and nearly silent when she walked, but in the mish mash of the forest her size was a hindrance. Sometimes.

Kaezanneth followed the path and emerged from the tree-line just as he went into the fishing shack. She laid down on the path and waited patiently to see where he would go next. After a few minutes she started to wonder just what he was doing with the bamboo stalk and the fishing rod. She was also perplexed that he hadn't headed for the village after reading the old sign. If she had been him, she would have gone there directly.

A sound within the shack prompted her to raise her head and glare at the doorway to the shack. The first noise was grunting followed by a tearing sound, and not just one long tearing sound. It was many tearing sounds that were short and very annoying. After hearing this for longer than she liked, the shack fell silent.

Kaezanneth sat up, now more curious than before, and crept in an arc away from the shack to try and get a view inside. The man-boy had taken the skin of the bamboo and tore it into very thin threads, then he braided them into a thin, long cord. He did this several more times until he had a considerable length of this thin cord. She watched as he threaded it through the tiny hoops on the rod and wrapped the remainder around a dowel on the opposite end.

The man-boy then took a lock of his hair and using a flat stone he found in the shack, cut it free of his scalp. He next tied the hair to the end of the cord then stood and turned to the doorway. He stopped abruptly and Kaezanneth realized that he did so because he saw her.

Like a shadow shrinking in the light she darted low, her belly nearly touching the ground and slipped back into the thicket along the forest edge. It was so fleeting that she hoped the man-boy would not be sure of what he saw.

Kaezanneth nimbly curved and curled her way amongst the branches and vines where she turned and peered through a bush full of tiny violet flowers back at him. The man-boy had rushed from within the shack to catch a glimpse of whatever the dark, four legged shape was that he saw.

She giggled under her breath at him. His head jerked left then right, but he could find nothing. He looked down at the sand thoughtfully and that is when she understood that he had found her foot-prints there. This did not worry her because he only studied the spot briefly then he went toward the water, raised the rod behind his head and cast the line over the gently rolling water of the lake.

Ah, so he is using his hair to bait a fish! she thought. Very clever, but not as much fun as gliding in the water and catching a fish in your teeth!

Time passed quickly and before she knew it he had caught a fish big enough to keep and he carried it back into the shack. She then heard a smacking sound and she knew he had used the flat rock to remove the head from the fish, and probably even scaled it as well. He came out of the shack, went into the forest, then returned with an armful of wood kindling and disappeared back into the shack. Before long he had somehow built a fire and she could smell the fish being cooked.

This man-boy was very, very clever, thought Kaezanneth, her mouth-watering for the taste of smoked fish. She looked up at the sky and the sun was now diving into the western horizon.

Had she been watching him all day?

She was thinking that she had seen enough of this stranger today, and now she wanted to go to her house and rest. She would return tomorrow and if the man-boy was still here, she would watch him some more. He was kind of interesting to observe, and he didn't act like any of the stories Arie's mother used to tell. Perhaps he was too young and hadn't been taught to be cruel yet. There was no way Arie's mother had told lies about the humans outside the valley. Arie's mother wouldn't have done that to Arie or her.

Kaezanneth shook her head again, trying to stave off the memories before they distracted her, and turned to leave. When she was deep enough into the forest and found a clearing, she spread her leathery, iridescent wings. They seemed to change colors in the waning sunlight from emerald to teal to lapis lazuli, a type of deep blue. It wasn't just her wings that had this quality. Each scale on her back and legs shifted colors depending on the way she moved. However, her underbelly skin was soft as a baby's and the color of milk.

With a few strong thrusts of her wings she left the ground like a cannonball from a cannon and sailed through the air with the grace of an eagle. Behind her, stretching for nearly the length of her body, was a slender tail with three fins at its end. Her colors shimmered as the light of the setting sun cascaded across the surface of her body.

Below Kaezanneth the tops of the forest trees zipped by effortlessly as she sailed through the air. The birds in the treetops squawked in protest and scattered at her passing like leaves in a strong wind. Lost in the moment she barrel-rolled around the tiny winged creatures before ascending then diving sharply at the winding river that divided the forest. She whizzed just inches above the water and dipped the tip of her nose leaving a trailing wake on the surface. Soon the trees lining the shore thinned out and before her was a vast overgrown grassland that ran as wide as the mountains.

Far away she could she the remains of her village, Springwater, and beyond that, looming over the jagged mountains was the peak of Mount Dayle, the largest in Ellamar.

Kaezanneth continued to follow the river as it snaked through the grassland, and before it curved to the east toward Springwater, she veered to the west. A mile away she could see a darkened collection of stones shaped like a farmhouse and the timber roof covering it. She landed into a full gallop on all fours and went to the house.

It was made of rough stone with timber framing around the door and windows, and the roof was aged and crumbling in places. The ground around the structure was hard clay and strewn about were broken and rotting farming tools. An ancient broken down wagon lay near one wall. The wheels had all but deteriorated down to the hub where the axles had rusted for what appeared to be hundreds of years.

This house, however dilapidated it may have been, was her house. It was also a place where she had been happiest in her entire life.

She walked around to the rear and headed to a spot thirty feet from the house where four large, misshapen rocks sat side by side. Scratched into each one was a name, although it was in the language of the dragons, and only she could read them, it was evident what their purpose was. She went to the smallest one belonging to Arie and kissed the name before turning and going back to the house.

The rear wall of the home had a large hole in it. She went through the hole and ducked her head and shoulders into the first room on the right. Inside the small room was a broken bed frame under a pile of tattered blankets that had once been used by Arie. Kaezanneth reached with one of her front feet, although they were actually hands, and she very carefully picked up a dirty child's doll on top of the blankets. The toy was barely held together by loose stitching and was on the verge of falling apart.

Cradling the tiny doll that had been Arie's, the dragon called Kaezanneth laid her head upon the old blankets. As she slipped into sleep she thought of how Arie had found her so long ago, and brought her to this house to meet her family. They welcomed her, cautiously at first, but soon the dragon was treated like she belonged and was even accepted by the citizens of Springwater, but Arie was her favorite. She loved the human-girl-child very much like a sister.

A smile found its way onto Kaezanneth's soft lips as she slept, but a few tears managed to escape from the young dragon's eyes.

8
THE AIRSHIP AND
THE ANGRY MEETING

ONE

The land below was a collage of textures and the colors of autumn as dirt roads, cobblestone homes with thatched roofs, leafy trees and lush fields of the last harvests of the season quickly passed under an oddity that was wholly unique in all the Nine Isles. Riding the sky as though it were a bird, with white sails trimmed in crimson, was the curved wooden hull belonging to a brigantine airship. It rode the air with such serenity it was as though it had never been in any sea in the Nine Isles. Quite to the contrary, at one time this ship did sail as other ships, but now it traveled the air as easily as any winged creature.

Unlike other airships, this brigantine did not use balloons of hot air to rise above the ground, nor did it use any mechanical means like wings or propellers to attain flight. Beneath the keel was a pocket of moving seawater that clung to the hull like it had been glued. The bow sliced through the infinite lapping waves, sending spectacular wings of blue and white spray splashing outward that disappeared into thin air. Behind the ship the water became opaque the further it got from the stern until it vanished from existence like a lifting fog.

Only the owner knew the reason and the origin of how such a vessel had been able to fly without balloons and propellers. Other airships in the Nine Isles needed those machinations to leave the earth, and even then they were nowhere near as fast and agile as this ship. This ship was certainly one of a kind, not unlike its captain.

Thareg Longtooth, the captain of the brigantine airship called The Skydancer, stood majestically on the quarterdeck, as still as a statue and of towering height, as he surveyed the eastern horizon. Flowing from under a wide and tall tricorne hat atop his head, was a luxurious tan mane that reached the wooden deck. His skin was covered in a soft hide, like that of a lion, and long whiskers poked outward from his cheeks. Protruding through his thick lips were the tips of four teeth that made his smile appear frightening when in fact he was not a frightening person. He was part of a race of cat-like people who called themselves the Aenthroghati.

Thareg was dressed in a cream colored tunic and a black longcoat with many pockets and buckles. The leggings he wore were loose fitting and a deep blue, ending at his bare feet whose resemblance to the paws of a lion was even more evident. From beneath bushy brown eyebrows were the most beautiful, and large, brown eyes.

"Skyvale dead ahead, Captain!" a gravelly voice boomed from above. In the distance was the white tower of the palace of Ellamar, rising above the sprawling city at the base of Mount Immanis.

Thareg turned his gaze to the top of the main mast where the voice came from. Clinging to the mast by a single hand and a heavy booted foot was a dwarf.

"Very good, Eochus! Helm, turn us three degrees starboard to Graymarch," Thareg ordered, his voice was like a soft growl.

The crewman at the helm steered the ship south-east as the dwarf released the mast and fell into the main sail. The thick cloth of the sail slowed his descent before landing on the deck with a mighty thud.

The dwarf was wide at the shoulder one-and-a-half times more than a man, very muscular, and had short, thick legs. His arms were long and ended in massive rough hands tipped with iron-strong fingernails. Covering his eyes was a pair of leather bound goggles fitted with black, irregular shaped lenses, strapped around his wide head with a leather strip. He was clad in buckled leather armor adorned with interlocking rings of silver covering much of the surface, and blackened animal hide pants tucked into his scuffed boots.

Eochus went directly to Thareg's side and gave him a heavy pat on the back. "So, Thareg, why've we come to Ellamar? It's way off our usual autumn course."

"Grimmholder's sister has need of us, my dwarf friend," the captain replied in earnest.

"Grimmholder has a sister? Younger, older?" Eochus asked.

"Does her age matter in the least, Eochus?" Thareg deflected the question, with a question.

"I just wanted to know how ugly she was," Eochus joked.

"I believe she is older my odd friend."

Eochus' nose crinkled. "That is rather ugly," he said with a hearty chuckle and he stomped down to the main deck where the crew was busy with preparing the ship for its landing approach.

"Eochus, answer me this, just how ugly are dwarf women again?" Thareg retorted playfully.

Eochus merely flashed his captain a smirk of contempt then went back to barking orders at the crew.

Thareg smiled wryly and chuckled.

The Skydancer's bow dipped toward the old fortress of Graymarch where it sat in the shadow of the South Cahannel Mountains.

The ancient stones of the fortress walls were riddled with markings from failed attempts to breach her defenses, and to this day no enemy had ever done so. The land around the fort was covered in autumn grass and trees whose leaves had begun to turn, but it was not always like this. There were long stretches of time when the ground was barren for months and even years because of idiotic battles from invading forces to take Graymarch. When those catastrophes had ended the land would grow and heal, until the next fracas would again decimate the earth.

Not far from the fortress was the humble, but no less grand, entrance to the Tomb of Lord Regents made of marble and granite.

As The Skydancer closed in on the fortress it was clear that there was bustling activity taking place within walls in the wide courtyard. A contingent of knights had started to move horses and wagons of equipment through the gate to meet the ship at the large stone ramp outside the fortress. Voices could be heard shouting to each other as preparations got underway to depart.

Following the line of knights and wagons were two women on horseback. One was dressed in white plate-mail armor and had striking red hair. She was also brandishing an elegant long sword on her hip. The other woman was frail by comparison, wearing a long weathered white frilled cloak and was being followed by numerous small, orange-winged butterflies. In her hand she had a staff that was nearly the length of her large pony.

The Skydancer sailed the air toward the ramp of stone, circled around it just two dozen feet above the congregation, then glided next to the ramp on the starboard side.

"Drop anchor!" Eochus' voice boomed the order and the ship's anchor plunged to the ground with a earthshaking thud.

A crewman rushed to the rail and removed a section of it for Thareg to step off the ship. Waiting for him on the ramp was the Knight of the March, a steward of the fortress, named Barnwell wearing a gleaming set of plate-mail armor.

"Welcome to Graymarch, Captain Longtooth. I am Barnwell, Knight of the March," Barnwell greeted with an outstretched hand.

Thareg wrapped his enormous three-fingered paw around Barnwell's hand and gently shook it. "Thank you, Barnwell. That is quite a title."

Barnwell nodded slightly.

Eochus swaggered up to Thareg's side and smiled wide, displaying his large, stained teeth.

Barnwell grimaced slightly at the dwarf, then said. "Right this way, captain. Lady Samarra is eager to speak with you."

"I do not understand, sir. I thought I was here to ferry the witch, Hildegrinnel," Thareg said.

"Yes sir, you are, as well as the lady and the Gray Knights," Barnwell said as he turned to lead Thareg and Eochus to Lady Samarra.

"What's all this now?" Eochus asked as he followed Thareg and Barnwell down the stone ramp, passing a number of wagons loaded with supplies and knights with their horses.

"I do not know, but I can say this, the Skydancer can not carry all that they have prepared," Thareg admitted.

"That's easily an understatement, captain," Eochus agreed.

Barnwell bowed upon reaching Lady Samarra and Hildegrinnel at the bottom of the loading ramp. "Lady Samarra, this is the captain of the Skydancer, and his dwarf."

"*His dwarf indeed,*" Eochus muttered to himself derisively.

Lady Samarra nodded to Barnwell and he turned quickly to continue his duties.

"My lady, I am Thareg Longtooth and my *dwarf,* Eochus Thorrium of North Hold, who is also my First Mate. May I say it is an honor to make your acquaintance."

"It is my honor as well, Captain Longtooth. Your reputation is well respected, from what I've been told. I also must apologize for Barnwell. He has no love for dwarves," Lady Samarra said to Eochus.

"He's not very attractive to me either!" Eochus spat.

Lady Samarra grinned at his words. "Very good, Mr. Thorrium. I agree."

"Please my lady, call me Eochus," the dwarf said to her with a coy smile.

Lady Samarra smiled for the first time since

Greggory had been taken from her at Eochus' flirtatious attempt. It was, however, a futile move for the dwarf. Her heart would never belong to another.

"My lady, time is not in abundant supply," Hildegrinnel added urgently.

"Of course, thank you Hildegrinnel," Lady Samarra said.

"My lady," began Thareg. "I came here under the pretense that Hildegrinnel alone needed the Skydancer, and I have yet to know the destination."

"Did my brother, Grimmholder, not explain that it was the Lady Samarra that you would be ferrying as well?" Hildegrinnel asked.

"No, Hildegrinnel, he did not. To be honest when we spoke he was not like himself," Thareg explained.

"His mind is no longer as focused as it once was. I do apologize, captain, but the Lady Samarra is who I asked you to ferry, along with the Gray Knights and our supplies. Can you do this?" Hildegrinnel asked.

"We can't take everything you have here! It's too much for the Skydancer!" Eochus told them excitedly.

Lady Samarra and Hildegrinnel looked to Thareg for his opinion of his first mate's claim. He nodded regretfully.

"My First Mate speaks the truth. The

Skydancer is too small to carry everything and everyone you wish," Thareg stressed.

Lady Samarra thought a moment, her commitment undeterred by this setback, then proposed an alternative, "Then we shall take only what we must absolutely cannot do without. Captain Longtooth, I will defer to your judgment. Look over my men and cargo and you tell me what your amazing airship can allow."

"I will do what I can, my lady," Thareg assured her, then looked to Eochus.

Eochus grinned and nodded his understanding, then took from a pocket a bit of graphite and a small parchment. He hurried off and began inspecting each parcel, wagon, horse and knight while scribbling onto the paper.

"Captain, what is your first mate doing?" Lady Samarra asked.

"Pardon me, my lady, but Eochus is a master of numbers as well as my first mate," Thareg explained. "He is estimating weights."

"Is he very good?' Lady Samarra asked, skeptical at such an absurdity as guessing weight.

"Oh yes, my lady. All dwarves are exceptional mathematicians," Thareg told her.

After several minutes Eochus returned to Thareg's side.

"Eochus, what have you to say?" Thareg asked his first mate.

"Well, captain, what I gathered from this

calamitous train of men and horses, the Lady Samarra will be able to take but five men, two horses and forty-stone of supplies," Eochus said firmly with a proud smile.

Thareg looked to Lady Samarra for her reaction.

Lady Samarra turned to Hildegrinnel, who nodded back. "That will be acceptable. Thank you Captain. Thank you Eochus," she thanked then called out, "Barnwell!"

Barnwell hurried back, bowed to Lady Samarra and said, "Yes, my lady?"

"Eochus has a list of what and who we will take aboard the airship. Follow it accordingly," Lady Samarra ordered.

"Yes, my lady," Barnwell said before taking the list from Eochus and looking it over.

"How long will it take you to have the ship loaded, Barnwell?" Lady Samarra asked the Knight of the March.

"No more than an hour, my lady," Barnwell said, then he hurried off to his work.

"Captain Longtooth, Eochus, shall we get aboard now?" Lady Samarra suggested.

"As you wish, my lady. Eochus would you lead the way?" Thareg asked.

"Don't you know the way, captain? The ship is just there at the top of the ramp." Eochus joked, pointing to The Skydancer.

Lady Samarra again smiled at the dwarf's

humorous remark. With any luck the journey to the Athenaeum would be just as pleasurable.

"My lady, where is it that I should set our course?" Thareg asked as he lead them toward the ramp and the Skydancer.

"Oh, of course, but it is not I that knows. Hildegrinnel, would you be so kind as to tell us all where we are to go?" Lady Samarra said.

Hildegrinnel nodded. "Make your course for the Crooked Mountains in Caledonia."

"The Crooked Mountains?" Eochus parroted back. "There's a lot of mountain, in those mountains."

"Master Eochus, our destination is not in the mountains. It is near a lake at the foot of those mountains," Hildegrinnel told them.

Thareg nodded to Hildegrinnel. "Caledonia it is."

TWO

Kaezanneth leaned her head over the edge of the rock ledge to look down, then cowered backward almost the instant she realized the depth to the bottom. She had gone to the highest point she could reach by walking to again try to alleviate her fear of heights.

It was ridiculous, of course, for a dragon to be afraid of heights, but nonetheless she was afraid. She could fly, but would do so just above the tops of the trees. Any higher and she would feel faint and get dizzy.

Every week since she had recovered from her accident, which trapped her in the valley, she would go to High Point Hill, the smallest peak in the chain of mountains surrounding Dayle, to try and break that fear. Today was no different. Her heart was pounding fiercely in her chest as the memory of her fall from the sky raced back into her mind. Her head began to feel like she was spinning causing her to lay down on the cool rocks.

This is stupid! she thought to herself. I'm a dragon! I should be able to fly as high as I want! she screamed at herself in thought.

Summoning her courage, she again crept to the edge and looked over. Just as before she reeled back from the precipice with a flutter in her heart.

When she awoke this morning she wanted to go and see the man-boy to spy on him, but she decided instead to come here first to test her fear. What she discovered was that she was still afraid of heights and it made her feel stupid.

She turned her attention away from the edge and looked out over the valley toward the lake beyond the Riverwood Forest.

A dragon's vision is a wondrous and remarkable thing. They can see in the night like it was day. The lightning fast wings of a humming-bird, through a dragon's eyes, move so slow that one could count the feathers easily. Great distances vanish in the eyes of a dragon like looking through a spyglass.

Kaezanneth could see the man-boy leaving the shack. He stopped to look around, as though he were trying to decide something, then stretched and yawned before walking toward the forest.

She raised her head quickly and stepped forward, watching with great curiosity. The man-boy stopped shy at the forest edge and appeared to be hesitant to enter.

What could be so hard about walking into the forest? What was he so afraid of? she thought. There isn't an animal within Riverwood that could harm him. What a goober!

Tilting her head in contemplation, she watched as he suddenly disappeared into the thicket of Riverwood. He was obviously heading for Springwater.

Kaezanneth stepped forward again, then her front leg-arms lost the ground from under them and she started to fall over the edge of the cliff. Panicked, her back legs dug into the stone with their thick, sharp claws trying to halt her slide.

She let out a shriek that echoed off the rocks and enveloped the valley. Her heart hammered against her ribcage the instant she gauged the distance to the ground. The world suddenly tumbled before her eyes as the fear overtook her senses. She hadn't fallen yet, but she felt as though it had happened.

Her eyes grew as wide as the moon when she started to slide ever more over the edge. Her claws tore gashes into the rock with a deafening screeching that scared the mountain birds from their nests. They flew like a swarm into Kaezanneth and before she could protest, her body succumbed to gravity.

She tumbled uncontrollably as she fell. The cliff-face whizzed by and she reached out to grab the stone. Her claws scratched the rock leaving a trail as she fell but was unable to get a good hold. Her leathery wings were tucked against her body, and she knew that if she didn't want to die she needed to open them. With the world spinning she could barely tell which way was up, but in the mish mash of colors she recognized the color of the ground and she had very little time. Summoning what courage she had left, she forced her wings open.

The rush of air filled the leathery membrane of her wings and they billowed to capacity. It was just enough to slow her fall and she managed to glide the last twenty feet until she crashed into the tops of the trees where she disappeared beneath the canopy. Branches snapped under her weight as she rocketed through the trees until she crashed and rolled on the forest floor with a loud series of thuds. Her screams frightened the birds and fleeing their nests, they scattered to the sky.

Every part of Kaezanneth's body that broke a branch or scraped the ground hurt like she had been twisted into a knot. She gingerly lifted herself, licked a spot on her leg that was bleeding and whined quietly. She tried to ignore the spinning sensation in her head. It wasn't just her body that was in pain. Her pride had been severely insulted when she plummeted through the treetops.

After testing her legs by bending and trotting in place for any serious injury, she galloped through the forest and out onto the plains between her and Springwater. She stopped and raised her head as high as her neck would allow to look over the tall grass, and could see the man-boy had just emerged from the woods near the town. In his hands she could see that he was carrying a long stick, and his steps toward the town were carefully measured.

Kaezanneth cocked her head and her scaly lips smiled wryly.

He's afraid, she thought with amusement and bolted with the quickness of a giant cat through the golden grasses of the plains toward Springwater.

Her streamlined body pierced the tall grass like a quiet whisper. Small field mice never heard her as she raced past them. The four-winged yellow yalat birds, who make their nests in the dense grasses, caught only fleeting glimpses of a blur as she leapt over them.

Before she knew it she had bounded from out of the tall grass on the opposite side of the river from the town. She slipped into the water without so much as a splash and with only the top of her head and eyes above the surface, she swam slowly to the other side. She crept from the river, careful to stay low and hid behind a stack of aging, rotting barrels next to a crumbling wall that was once the ale-root brewery. Through the cracks in the wall she could she the man-boy as he cautiously made his way into town.

He suddenly stopped and stared in her direction before she realized she was breathing so hard he could hear. She held her breath and waited. Steam began to rise from her body as the water evaporated from the heat she was expelling, like a hot stove.

After a moment he began to walk again…

THREE

Rikter slowly made his way along the earthen road that ran through, what he assumed, was the center of the town.

The masonry in the buildings lining the road were cracked and crumbling from years of neglect.

Their roofs, some thatched, some overlapping wooden or stone tiles, were plagued with holes of varying sizes. The most unfortunate building's roofs were completely decayed. Tall weeds lined the edges of the walls and leafy, twisted vines climbed and snaked their way through the cracks.

Along the road were at least a dozen broken down wagons with rotting wheels and rusted filings that had been unused for what looked like decades. Some had boxes and burlap bags still loaded and were covered in layers of dirt and had been swallowed by tall weeds.

Darkened windows stared at Rikter as he passed each structure sending a chill up his young spine. The town looked completely abandoned the deeper he explored.

Where were the townsfolk? Why did they abandon their homes and shops? Did they abandon the town or was there another reason for their absence? These were the thoughts running inside Rikter's confused mind.

When he reached the town's square, where a dry fountain made of rough stone sat, he was able to see down three other roads. At the end of the east road he could see the remains of a church. Beside it was a very crowded cemetery harboring more gravestones than there was room, with some of those stones planted in the road.

The sight of the gravestones unsettled him.

"Hello!" Rikter called out hopelessly but his

voice only disappeared into the unresponsive wind. "Hello! Is there anybody here?"

Nobody responded to the teenager's call, and nobody would.

From a dilapidated blacksmith shop, spying on Rikter through a gap under a rusted anvil on a large, flattened stone, was Kaezanneth. She had been following him, ducking between buildings and slipping through holes in the walls to keep out of his eyesight.

She was very curious about him. He still didn't behave like the stories Arie's mother had told. He hadn't fashioned any weapons nor was he wearing any armor. Then again he had only been in her valley for two days.

When he had called out she did feel a little sorry for him, but only a moment. He was alone, like her, but she couldn't show herself just yet. It was too soon and she wanted to be absolutely sure of his intentions.

Rikter leaned into one of the shops in the square, his stick poised to strike any danger lurking in the gloom, and again called, "Is there anyone here? Hello! My name is Rikter!"

His name is Rikter? What kind of name is Rikter? It sounds like it belongs to a pet, like a dog or cat! Kaezanneth thought. Human names always sound weird.

Rikter returned to the fountain and sat on the stone ring surrounding it. He drooped his head and he sighed with disappointment. "There's nobody here."

He began doodling in the dirt road with the stick. The hope of civilization here had vanished like smoke in a strong wind.

He looked to the north road where it shrank into the horizon below a behemoth mountain that rose above the range of imposing rock. The western road led to a bridge over the river and in the distance, on a lonely but small rise in the land, was the shape of a tiny house.

For whatever reason, Rikter wasn't sure why, he decided he would go there with the hope of finding someone. He stood, squared his shoulders with renewed hope, and started for the bridge. He looked to the sky for the sun and found it directly overhead, so he had plenty of time before nightfall. If need be he would stay the night in the house on the hill.

Kaezanneth watched Rikter go to the bridge and cross it. She understood right away where he was going, and the sneer on her lips made it clear she didn't like it.

He's going to MY house! she thought angrily.

Kaezanneth darted from behind the anvil with the surefootedness of a cat and dashed toward the river. This time rather than swim across she leapt, spread her wings, and silently glided over the water. She landed without a sound and slunk into the tall grass.

In the corner of Rikter's eye he saw movement, but when he looked Kaezanneth had already melded with the golden grass as it swayed in the wind. Was there something there? He wondered, then remembered the dark shape on the beach that had mysteriously vanished the other day. He also recollected the large footprints in the sand.

Was whatever he saw on the beach real? If so, was it here too, perhaps following him? If there was a creature in this valley, was it dangerous or curious? It would be reasonable to say that if it was dangerous, would it have already attacked and eaten him?

He wanted to be afraid, but after reasoning that if it was a predator he would already be dead, he decided he no longer needed the stick. He tossed it into the field then continued along the dirt path toward the lonely house on the hill.

Kaezanneth stalked Rikter from within the grass as he walked up the dirt road to the house. The closer he got the more agitated she became. She didn't want to have to chew him up for invading her home, if he did, and he had gotten rid of the stick so it would be much easier to do so. Also, she had never 'chewed' anyone before and wasn't sure she would find it appealing.

If he did anything to disrespect her home she would find out just what human tasted like, and she hoped it wasn't nasty.

Rikter slowly approached the house, taking notice of the strewn, useless tools and the ruined wagon in the yard. Scattered on the ground in front of the house were the bones of small animals. The inside of the house was mostly in shade, in part to the roof not being as decayed as some of the others in town. He stopped and noticed the large three-toed footprints in the soft clay. They looked like the ones on the beach when he studied them.

Was the creature here? he thought.

He lowered himself and touched the impression. It was hardened. He guessed it was at least a day old.

Kaezanneth watched closely as he looked at her footprint. He knows how to track! She thought. That's just great! Now how am I supposed to keep an eye on him?

He stood and peered into the window of the house. "Hello, is anybody here?" he asked, not expecting any response just like before. Looking around briefly, he went to the open doorway and leaned inside. The front room floorboards had deteriorated leaving the hard clay in its place and the fireplace hearth had collapsed. Cobwebs filled the corners of the room like lace doilies of fine silk. The smell of stale earth filled Rikter's nose as he went inside, careful to step over the hearthstones littering the ground.

Uh! He went inside! Kaezanneth screamed inside her mind. He went INSIDE! How rude!

She silently rushed toward her home, stopping at the wall, then as carefully as she could muster, climbed onto the roof. A rafter inside the house creaked under her weight and she froze nervously.

Uh oh, she thought.

Rikter's heart jumped in his chest when he heard the wood groan over his head. His eyes darted to the ceiling as dust rained down in front of his face. "Is anyone here?" He said loudly. When nothing more happened he continued his search of the house. He followed a short hallway with a doorway on the left and right, but more noticeable than that was the large hole in the back wall leading outside. He walked the length of the hall and stopped just outside under the warm sun.

Rikter stared befuddled at four large upright stones with strange markings a short walk from the house. He walked to the stones then took notice of three grass mounds at the foot of each stone. He stopped abruptly.

The stones were marking graves, he realized. It sent a wave of sadness through his heart.

Kaezanneth peered over the roof ridge and watched Rikter as he went to the stones. She sneered.

He better not touch any of them, she thought. "Oh my," Rikter muttered to himself. He slowly backed away from the three markers and went back inside the house through the hole. Kaezanneth peeked over the ridge of the roof and stretched her neck over the edge to watch him just as he went into Arie's room.

Kaezanneth felt a surge of contempt run up her spine. He's in Arie's room! She raged silently then climbed back to the ground and went to the window of Arie's room, careful to peek in.

Rikter cautiously went into the room on the right. Inside he found a broken bed covered with tattered blankets, and resting on them was an old, dirty child's doll. The rest of the room was like the front room, cobwebs in the corners and the stale smell of earth and stone.

He leaned down and looked at the doll, curious for a moment. There were three gravestones outside. Wouldn't it make sense that they would be for two parents and a child? Also, wouldn't it make sense that a child would've been laid to rest with their favorite toy?

Kaezanneth's eyes narrowed with impending hostility. He was too close to Arie's doll and her blood was beginning to boil with anger.

He picked the doll up with great care, but it meant nothing to the large, dragon outside who was watching him closely. The window frame was suddenly filled with the head and neck of a snarling, snapping dragon. The frame snapped and the stone wall encasing it buckled as she tried to reach Rikter to chew on him. Dust rained from the ceiling as her struggling shook the roof and the walls. She clawed the wall from outside as she tried to force her body through the window opening, but for her slim physique she was still too large to get through.

"MONSTER!" Rikter cried out.

He fell backward in a terrible panicked state, clutching the doll to his chest and screaming like a frightened child. The drumming of his heart filled his ears with the sound of blood flying through his veins. The dragon's hot breath on his face smelled foul and stung his eyes.

Rikter scrambled backward out of the room where he managed to stand and blindly run into the front room where he tripped over a hearthstone. He slammed into the hard clay knocking the wind from his lungs.

Kaezanneth yanked her head from the window and rushed around to the hole in the back wall where she was just in time to watch Rikter fall. She hurried inside but the narrow walls prevented her from entering the front room. She let fly a deafening roar that split the air and snapped at his feet with deadly teeth, but he was just out of reach.

Rikter screamed again with his stomach in his throat, and scampered to his feet. He ran for the doorway and as before, he tripped on the stoop and somersaulted outside.

Kaezanneth watched him fall again, and she couldn't help but snicker. He had fallen twice and she never actually was able to bite him.

Is he a klutz? she asked herself in thought.

Kaezanneth backed out of the house and went around the side, but instead of chasing him, she leaned around the corner. She watched as he climbed to his feet.

Rikter looked back and saw her looking at him. "By the divines!" he shouted.

Kaezanneth grinned widely at him, showing off her long, pointed teeth in a display meant to be somewhat friendly, but to him it had an opposite effect. He gasped with fright and bolted away without taking his eyes off her.

Rikter was in such a panic to get away that he ran into the wagon and fell headlong into the back of it.

Yep, he's a klutz, Kaezanneth thought again, then cocked her head and giggled at him. She hadn't moved toward him and he was falling all over everything trying to get away.

He awkwardly tried to climb out of the back of the wagon but an old rope that was in the back wrapped itself around him like living tentacles. The edge of the carriage caught his foot as he fought with the rope and he tumbled over the edge onto the hard ground. He jumped up still fighting with the rope then looked around. The dragon was looking right at him with a wide tooth-filled grin. Without a thought, the panic again overtook him easily and he let out another wheezy scream. He began running down the path to the town dragging a length of the rope still wrapped around an ankle.

Yep. He's a BIG klutz, she thought.

Her anger toward him touching Arie's doll was replaced with mild amusement. She went to the wagon to retrieve the doll but it wasn't there. He hadn't dropped it. Her head snapped up and she looked at him as he reached the bridge. In his hand she could see Arie's doll. Her lip curled with malicious and mischievous intent as she galloped after him.

9

THE SISTERS...AGAIN

"The dragon tried to eat him!" Wisdom cried. "Why did she try to eat him?" She looked to Fate, whose true name was Amandonia, with a confused expression.

Amandonia looked back at Caroleythia, divine of wisdom, then stared back out the window. "Did she eat him?"

"No, but she tried."

A blue-bird landed on the sill and Amandonia gracefully lowered a hand. The little bird hopped onto a finger and chirped. "He still lives, does he not?"

"Yes."

Courage, Angellevere, paced between the two of them in deep thought. "Are we not done with the boy? There are others in the world we have to attend to. Is this not true?"

"I agree. We can return to the boy after he has left Ellamar," said Gwendelor, the divine of chance, who was sitting by the warmth of the fireplace. "Amandonia, what do you see for the Lady and her entourage? Do they survive their journey to Caledonia?"

"Yes. They arrive in the land of the elves, but do so after a great struggle, wouldn't you agree?" Amandonia asked as she gently petted the bird before it returned to the air on tiny wings.

"I do agree, and I foresee a battle with two great beasts of the earth, but I do not see the outcome," Gwendelor declared.

"Of course you don't see the outcome!" Angellevere barked. "All you see is the events before they occur! Amandonia sees the outcome!"

"Do you think I don't know this, sister?" Gwendelor hissed back.

"I sometimes wonder what you know if anything!" Angellevere heckled her.

"Angellevere, you've been more agitated than I have ever seen you. What vexes you so?" Caroleythia asked.

"I have noticed this as well," Amandonia added calmly.

"I have not, and if I have been, do you not see the darkness coming? It will not only destroy the world, but we Divines as well!" Angellevere claimed anxiously.

"We have done all that we are permitted," Gwendelor told her. "Or have you forgotten what father decreed?"

"No I have not, but why does father ignore the signs? I am worried that our manipulations may not be enough," Angellevere admitted.

"What do you suggest?" Caroleythia asked.

Angellevere traded looks with each sister. "We could ask for help from the others."

"How can you say that when only two days ago you scolded Aembresculathia for aiding the boy in Dayle?"

Angellevere lowered her eyes from their gaze in shame. "Perhaps I was…hasty?"

"You mean wrong, do you not, sister?" Gwendelor said, grinning with satisfaction.

"I was not wrong…then," Angellevere snapped back.

"We cannot ask for help. Father will see and would punish us," Amandonia said.

"I suppose you saw that, too!" Angellevere said sharply.

"I did, sister."

"Oh, then, very good Amandonia," Angellevere conceded reluctantly.

"Isn't anyone going to mention the horrible voice in the clouds above Skyvale that killed the serpine assassin? Should we not try to discover who that was?" Caroleythia suggested.

Without warning the ice crystal sphere at the center of the room lit up with a soft white light that stole their attention. The feeling that surrounded the sisters gave them a sense of safety and love. Then a voice spoke to them from within the crystal.

"My daughters of destiny. I hear your worries." The voice was deep, but soothing.

The sisters all fell to one knee and bowed their heads.

"Father," Began Angellevere, "Have we angered you?"

"No, Angellevere, you have not. The four of you, however, have been plotting something. Have you not?"

"No Father, we have not been plotting," Caroleythia said. "We have done what we have been allowed to do, by your word."

There was a brief silence that made them all nervous, then he spoke again, "Is this true, Angellevere?"

Angellevere looked to each sister, as was her habit in times of indecision, then answered, "Yes Father, in a way."

"Explain this 'way'."

Gwendelor touched Angellevere on a shoulder and nodded to her. "I will tell him. Father, I used the Worm of Yeningregger to hasten a young boy's destiny."

"I see. I am not amused with the awakening of the worm before it is time. The balance has been upset by this," their Father's voice said firmly. "Was this boy so important that you had to summon that vile creation of Tahnazuu?"

Caroleythia spoke up anxiously, "Yes, Father, he is! His name is Rikter Waycross, and he is needed to keep Bahraam imprisoned!"

Their Father sighed with annoyance. "Are you on about this again, my daughters? If it Bahraam's time to return, then it will happen."

"I do not believe so, Father," Amandonia declared, her voice quivering. "I have seen the end of Rikter Waycross's story, and he will prevail against Bahraam. You must allow us…"

"I am the Father, and I will do what I wish, my daughters. You are my children and you will obey my commands."

"Even if it destroys the world?" Angellevere asked sternly.

"The world is not eternal, Angellevere," their Father began with a tenderness to his tone. "It will come to an end one day, and so shall we," he continued, "I do not wish for Bahraam to return, but the races of the Nine Isles sealed him away, and it is their calamity to endure. If they are strong, if they unite and put aside all their hatred of one another, they may yet put an end to Bahraam, but they will do so without the Divine's interference. They have only themselves to look to for victory. So I say this, to all four of you, and I will tell your other siblings the same; No more will you intervene directly with Rikter Waycross than you have already done. Perform your duty as you were given but do not appear before any creature upon the Nine Isles. That is my word and as such is law."

The sisters of destiny exchanged downtrodden looks such as a child scolded would, then said together, "Yes Father."

As quickly as the penetrating light had originated, it faded away and left them staring into their blank ice crystal. Heavy was their despair as they lost all their words, and it would have ended their schemes had it not been for Angellevere who spoke next.

"Did Father say not to interfere anymore?" Angellevere asked rhetorically.

"Yes, I do believe he did," Gwendelor said.

Caroleythia and Amandonia nodded to her.

"He did," Angellevere said, her wheels of conniving spinning wildly. "But he also said, in that same sentence, not to interfere DIRECTLY with Rikter Waycross." She grinned deviously.

"What horrible idea is twisting inside your head, sister?" Caroleythia asked.

"We cannot directly interfere with Rikter," Angellevere stated.

"Yes that is what Father said," Gwendelor agreed.

"What is it you are trying to tell us, sister?" Amandonia asked.

"Who is it that we know disobeys Father at every opportunity, and would be willing to get involved if the chance of battle were impending?" Angellevere asked.

Gwendelor suddenly gasped with the answer, her eyes lighting up with renewed excitement. "Marthandiel!"

"Exactly!" chimed Angellevere.

"Oh no. Not Marthandiel, sisters!" pleaded Caroleythia. She went to Angellevere and took her hands in her own. "Please, do not drag him into this! He will surely run afoul all of our efforts!"

"You must have faith, Caroleythia," Gwendelor tried to reassure her.

"Very well, I have faith that Marthandiel will run afoul of all our efforts," Caroleythia mocked.

"You needn't worry about Marthandiel, dear Caroleythia," Amandonia said softly and all eyes turned to her. She had walked away from the conversation to the window.

Angellevere went to her side. "What do you mean by that, sister?"

Caroleythia and Gwendelor looked on with curiosity.

"You do not know?" Amandonia asked.

"No we do not. If we did I would not have asked you the meaning of your statement, now would I?" Angellevere snapped.

"Marthandiel has not been seen since the Battle at the Tower of Light," Amandonia said. "Almost two thousand years ago."

"Then we shall find him," Angellevere said, her tone dire.

"I will begin the search immediately," said Gwendelor and she went to the crystal where she gazed upon the world for their lost brother.

10
STRANGE FRIENDS

ONE

Rikter's heart was still hammering in his chest and his mind racing with the horrendous thought of being eaten as he ran toward town. Ahead of him was the bridge crossing the river and with it the hope of hiding from the monster he thought was chasing after. There was no chance he could outrun Kaezanneth, but still he ran as fast as he could while blindly clutching the doll. Had he not been in a panic he would have felt the rope still wrapped around his ankle that was dragging along the dirt road.

Kaezanneth's feet pounded the earth as she bolted toward Rikter. Etched on her face was a devious grin at what she was about to do, and it made her more eager to do it.

Just as Rikter reached the middle of the bridge, the dragon stomped on the rope wriggling on the ground with a powerful foot. Rikter suddenly fell forward when the rope became taut. He slammed onto the wooden planks with a loud, painful thud, like a tree falling in the woods.

Rikter let out a whimper as all the air in his lungs was forced from him from the very hard fall. As he rolled onto his back he became aware of a strange sound. It was like a hiccup and a growl all at once. He sat up slowly, his arms across his aching chest, and saw the monster on the dirt road. It was rollicking around on the dusty road, kicking up dirt as it did so.

Kaezanneth laughed as dragons do, with a hearty growling chuckle, as she rolled on the ground. She hadn't laughed like that in a very long time, and she really enjoyed it.

Rikter cocked his head as he watched Kaezanneth, who just then stopped on her back and stared at him, her head upside down. Her mouth widened in an attempted smile, brandishing two rows of pointed teeth, that only added to Rikter's fear. She then scrambled upright and dashed into the tall grass again.

Was it laughing at him? Why hadn't this large creature killed him already? Was it even trying to kill him, or was it toying with him like a cat does to a mouse before eating it?

These thoughts flashed through Rikter's mind as he furiously untied the rope, snatched the doll with a hand and ran into town. He passed the dry fountain and headed down the south road that brought him from the lake.

Where could he go so this creature could not find him? It obviously lived in that house he had discovered in the field, and that being the truth, it also probably knew every square mile of this valley trapped by mountains.

A sound overhead snatched Rikter back to

reality and made him cringe. Then a large shadow flashed across the ground in front of him. He looked up to catch a glimpse of Kaezanneth as she jumped from one roof to another. Tiles rained down from the crumbling rooftops.

Did it have wings? he thought. He was sure he saw wings as it jumped overhead.

Rikter ducked between two ruined homes and continued along the narrow street as quickly as his tired legs could muster. His chest began to hurt with every breath as he pushed himself to flee. Then another shadow draped him in shade as Kaezanneth bounded from another rooftop over him. He turned again and hurried up another street.

Directly ahead of him he caught the site of Kaezanneth as she leapt onto the top of a three story, dilapidated storehouse. When she touched down on the roof it broke beneath her feet and she disappeared into the ruin, letting out a desperate cry. The sound of wooden floors cracking and stone crumbling filled the air and a cloud of dust exploded, encasing the area in a thick, gray shroud.

Rikter slowed, unable to see. When the dust settled he saw Kaezanneth's head poking through a hole in the wall only a few feet from him. She shook the dirt from her head, then grinned at him like an embarrassed child. He flinched with a gasp and ran back the way he had come.

What is he so afraid of? Kaezanneth asked

herself in thought. I'm not trying to chew him anymore. Does he not know this? Not only is he a klutz and a goober, he's also some kind of wandering idiot!

Kaezanneth burst through the hole in the wall and climbed to the roof of another building. She sailed through the air from one roof to another as before, following Rikter as he tried to get away. He had slowed considerably from fatigue and it was now time to get back her property.

As Rikter turned another corner he was drowned in a shadow that grew larger and larger.

"Uh oh!" he stammered then turned to look upward just as Kaezanneth pounced on him. He let loose a high pitched scream that could've broken glass.

Kaezanneth roared fiercely in Rikter's face at the top of her lungs, her mouth wide enough to swallow his head in a single gulp. Her white teeth were as long as a man's finger, and she had a tongue fat enough to smother him. Fanning outward from her back with grand finesse, was the full breadth of her wings that swallowed them in shadow.

He threw up his arms to cover his head with the child's doll still in one hand. His whole body trembled with fear as he cried out, "PLEASE DON'T EAT ME!"

Kaezanneth snapped her mouth shut and

cocked her head at him. She pressed her slim snout into his arms until he parted them enough for her to see his face. Her nose was nearly touching his as she looked deep into his terrified brown eyes. There was something in those eyes that she understood. Something meaningful and warm and honest just behind the fear he was feeling right now, that only her kind could see. It was as if she was judging his very soul, and in that instant she saw what she needed. It reminded her of Arie.

She reared her head back and said to him, "I'm not going to eat you. I don't have any ketchup."

Rikter's brow furrowed with confusion.

It spoke? He didn't know monsters could speak.

Kaezanneth gently reached toward him with a hand, and with great care took the doll from him with the tips of her claws.

"Not yours. This is Arie's," she said in a voice that was soft and not what he had expected. She then backed away and turned to leave.

Rikter's chest had been rattling as his heart raced, but now it began to calm when he realized he wasn't going to be eaten. He cautiously lowered his arms just enough to see her better. "I'm sorry. I didn't know," he said timidly. "Who is Arie?"

Kaezanneth kept walking away, coddling

Arie's doll to her chest. "Arie is my sister."

Rikter's eyes narrowed. "Who are you?"

"I'm Arie's sister," she told him, deliberately being obscure.

Rikter sighed. "My name is…"

"I know your name. It's Rikter," she cut him off.

How did she know my name? he thought, then asked, "How do you know my name?"

Kaezanneth spun her head around at him, and with her free hand she wriggled her four fingers in a wave at him. "I can read minds," she joked.

Rikter shuddered at the thought of this large creature being able to read his mind. "Can you?"

"Of course not," she continued, "I heard you say your name in the town store. You're a goober."

Goober? Rikter said in his thoughts. What kind of word is goober?

Kaezanneth turned away again and started walking back toward the center of town.

Rikter sat up. "I'm lost. Can you tell me where I am?"

"I can," she replied.

Rikter waited for her to answer but she kept walking until she rounded a corner and disappeared from sight. He stood and limped after her on sore, bare feet. He turned the same corner and saw her near the fountain.

"Well?" he called out.

"Well what?"

"Can you tell me where I am?"

"I can," she repeated.

"Then please can you tell me where I am?" he pleaded.

"I would, but you need to ask the right question."

"I don't understand," he told her. His patience was beginning to wane.

"You asked if I can, but not if I will," she enlightened him.

Rikter's mouth fell open when he understood. "Ah, you're teasing with me, aren't you?"

"Aren't you a smart one?"

Rikter sighed, frustrated. Of all the creatures in the world, he had to get one with not only a sense of humor, but a sassy attitude as well. "Okay, I'll play along. Will you tell me where I am? Please?"

"You're behind me, silly," Kaezanneth told him, again teasing.

"That's not what I meant!" Rikter huffed.

"But it is what you asked." Kaezanneth chuckled as she began to cross the bridge leading out of town.

"This valley, what is it called?"

Kaezanneth stopped abruptly and turned to look at him. The corner of her mouth was upturned in a half grin. "It is called Dayle, and it is my home."

Rikter limped to the bridge and sat on the ground. His feet hurt and he was covered in dirt, smelled foul, and was very sweaty. "Dayle? The Lost Valley of Dayle?"

"It's not lost. I know exactly where it is because it's under us. I'm going to my house now. Do not follow me. You are not invited," Kaezanneth said to him before turning and walking away.

"Wait. If this is Dayle, the Dayle of legend, then I must be in Ellamar!" Rikter said excitedly.

"I don't know where Ellamar is and I don't care."

"How do you not know where you are? What sort of creature are you?" Rikter demanded of her, very cross.

"You didn't know where you were until I told you! And I am not a *creature*, I am a dragon, man-boy!" Kaezanneth said tersely.

"My name is Rikter!" he yelled back.

Kaezanneth shook her head. "I know, but I don't like your name. I am going to call you Goober from now on."

Rikter gawked. "What the heck is a goober?"

TWO

Rikter spent the night on the floor of the fishing shack, shivering against the chill of the autumn night. When he awoke the next morning he was covered in an old blanket riddled with small holes, obviously caused by field mice. In spite of the holes, the blanket managed to keep him very warm.

Did the dragon place the blanket over him last night? When he returned to the shack late yesterday afternoon he was alone the entire time he fished and ate his catch, and the dragon was nowhere near.

Rikter didn't know what to think about the dragon, partly because she had tried to munch on him, and the other part was because he had never seen a dragon before. She also acted like she didn't like him very much when she said he wasn't invited to her home, so why would she provide him with a blanket?

He muddle over those thoughts for a minute then sat up and stretched. He then threw the blanket over an arm and stood. After grabbing the fishing rod, he slowly lumbered out of the shack.

The morning sun had just climbed over the summit of the mountain range forcing the cold of the night to retreat for another day. Rikter lifted his face toward the sky allowing the rays to kiss his skin before he turned to the woods and followed the path to the town.

When he made it to Springwater he went into the shop across from the dry fountain where he had called out his name. Inside he found that the floor was mostly intact and the store shelves were mostly in one piece. He draped the blanket over a broken chair and leaned the fishing pole against the wall. He then left the shop and looked around for someplace that had a bed.

What caught his attention first was the dragon laying on the ground on the other side of the river, watching him. Her front legs were crossed and her long, winged tail lazily flopped side to side behind her.

What was she doing now? He thought she made it clear she wasn't very fond of him.

Rikter hobbled along the street, ducking into one ruin after another until he found an old straw mattress. He dragged it back to the shop, laid it down and slid the shelves so that it was hidden from one side. It was then that his stomach growled loudly to be fed.

Rikter took the fishing rod and went outside. The dragon was still watching him from afar as he walked to the river's edge and cut another lock of his hair to use as a lure. He tied it to the line and looked at the dragon.

Kaezanneth rolled her eyes and sighed, then she stood and walked across the bridge. She turned toward him and trotted past, careful to keep her distance. She didn't want him to think she liked him or was even comfortable with him. Not yet.

"You're not going to catch any fish in that river, Goober," she said as she went into the field of tall grass.

Rikter kept an eye on her as she bounded through the grass like she was playing some odd game. "The river goes to the lake, doesn't it?"

"Yes!" she shouted back.

Rikter thought a moment then said, "So if there is fish in the lake, shouldn't the river also have fish?"

"One would think so!"

Rikter smirked at her remark. She was very cryptic. So much so that it was maddening. Were dragons like that? He wouldn't have that knowledge because he had never known a dragon before her. What did she know about rivers and lakes or even fish, for that matter? He was a sailor, and sailors lived on the sea, and fish are in the sea. So therefore he was an expert at all things in the water, and she was a dragon, a creature of the sky, and surely she didn't know anything about the sea or the animals in it.

"We'll just see if I catch a fish in this river," he said confidently and he cast the line into the water.

As the hours passed without incident, Rikter sat on the ground and felt his confidence drain away. Surely something would eventually bite the lure and be hooked, but this did not happen. The sun slowly crossed the sky until it had reached the western horizon, and still nothing tampered with Rikter's fishing line.

He propped the rod up using a pair of forked twigs and gingerly looked at his feet. They were in such pain that they burned like they were on fire, and he saw why. Blisters had begun to form on his soles and a few were bleeding. All the running he did yesterday had taken their toll. If only he had his boots.

When the sun dropped below the mountains the darkness and chill of night returned. Rikter reeled in his line and went back to the shop where he laid the rod beside the doorway. Next to that he found a vine creeping up the wall with small wild berries growing on it. He gathered them up and put them in an old wooden bowl he found on a shelf.

Rikter then gathered some stones that were lying nearby and formed them into a circle inside the shop near the doorway before breaking one of the shelves to use for firewood.

Before long the shop was drowning in the warm glow of a fire. Rikter sat on the straw mattress with the blanket over his shoulders as he ate the berries. They weren't bad even though their taste was a little tart.

Kaezanneth happened by a short time later

and followed the light of the fire to the doorway. In her jaws were three rabbits she had caught in the field. Without a word she turned and headed home.

THREE

The next morning Rikter again walked to the river on sore feet, this time to a spot further north of the bridge but still close to the shop. Just as he was about to cast his line he saw Kaezanneth. She was on the bridge into town, sitting on her haunches with her arms crossed. The expression on her face looked like disappointment.

Rikter nodded at her but she did nothing in response. He cast his line into the clear water and propped the rod using the sticks from yesterday. When he looked at her she lowered and shook her head, then walked his way again.

As she passed him to head into the fields, she said in a brash tone, "You're not going to catch any fish in this river from that spot either, Goober."

"I believe I will, and my name is Rikter!" he replied in a huff.

"That's a stupid name, Goober," Kaezanneth teased then disappeared into the field of tall grass.

Rikter ignored her and settled onto the ground holding the fishing rod. "This may be her home, but I know how to fish," he muttered to himself.

The day went by almost as quickly as yesterday, and with each hour Rikter lost a little more hope in catching anything. He kept a loose eye on the dragon as she milled about in the fields, obviously hunting small animals like before. It was like she was enjoying his failure to fish effectively while gloating about her ability to hunt.

After another few hours Rikter found himself pacing along the river's edge, kicking the occasional pebble into the water. When his feet began to hurt too badly he sat on the ground near the waters' edge and dipped them into the river. The cold water provided some relief.

A few times during the day he caught Kaezanneth watching him nurse his blistered feet and she quickly turned away feigning disinterest. Most of the time he kept his attention glued to the fishing rod. Not once during the day did it bob to tell him he had a nibble.

When the sun dove behind the mountains, Rikter reeled in his line, slung the rod near the shop doorway and collected more small berries to eat by the fire. Sitting on the mattress with the blanket around his shoulders he sulked at his failure. To make it worse the dragon soon trotted toward the bridge on the way to her house. In her mouth dangled three fat snakes she had managed to catch.

She looked at him through the shutter-less window, lowered her head dejectedly and walked away.

FOUR

Rikter's third morning living in the shop in Springwater started like the previous mornings. He awoke, wrapped the blanket around himself, and hobbled outside to greet the sun. This time however there was a pair of antiquated, time worn boots sitting on the fountains edge. He limped to the fountain and picked one up. In spite of them being more than a hundred years out of style, they were in considerably good condition. He felt inside and the padding on the soles was intact.

He quickly scanned around him to see if the dragon was nearby, watching him perhaps, but she was nowhere to be seen.

The dragon must've been responsible for giving him the boots just like she had given him the blanket three nights ago. Why was she helping him but treating him with such indifference? Was this the way dragons behaved? He had no way of knowing anything about her or dragons. There was hardly anyone in the world who even knew what a dragon looked like, let alone how they behaved. Dragons disappeared from the Nine Isles over three hundred years ago.

This dragon, if that was what she was, acted like she had no interest in speaking, but she was always nearby. She was watching him and critiquing him as he tried to fish, and now she was giving him boots?

Rikter sat on the ground and put the boots on his sore, blistered feet. He stood and took a few steps, and when the pain wasn't as bad as it had been he smiled with relief. He took a moment to look around for the dragon but she wasn't anywhere near him. Not yet.

Rikter hurried to get his fishing rod, tossed the blanket onto the mattress and grabbed a handful of the berries from last night. He then rushed to the riverbank and instead of using his hair, he strung several berries to the bamboo line.

He felt renewed hope that was brought on by having boots on his feet, and swung the rod over a shoulder to cast. He stopped suddenly when he saw something dark sitting to his left. He looked to see the dragon laying on the ground, arms crossed, scrutinizing him just a dozen feet away.

Rikter stared at her, frozen in her gaze. "What am I doing wrong, now?" he asked.

"Good morning, Goober," Kaezanneth greeted him.

Rikter's face went blank. "Good morning?"

"Are you using those berries to try and catch fish today?" Kaezanneth asked.

"Uh, yes," Rikter stammered.

"Okay, but you will still be unable to catch any fish in the river, even with the berries," Kaezanneth told him.

"Is that so?" Rikter asked.

Kaezanneth nodded. "Especially with the berries. Those things taste horrible!"

"I've been eating them for two days now. They don't taste bad at all," Rikter admitted.

"Okay, if you say so."

They stared at each other for a while before Rikter spoke.

"I'm going to fish now," he said.

Kaezanneth nodded to him.

Rikter cast his line and the dragon sighed, then planted her face into a palm. She stood and swaggered past him on her way to the fields.

"You're not going to catch…" she began but Rikter interrupted her by finishing her thought.

"…Any fish in the river. Yes, I know, I know," Rikter mocked. When she vanished into the tall, grassy field he propped the rod with the forked sticks and made himself comfortable on the ground.

The day sluggishly lumbered by, as it does while waiting for something to happen, especially while fishing, and he waited in silence. Puffy white clouds rolled overhead like giant balls of cotton and the sun crawled across the blue fabric of the sky with lazy abandon. A light breeze danced in the grass and trees, both warm and cool. Birds chirped as they flew through the air in search of food, and somewhere in the distance the sound of Kaezanneth bounding in the field scaring up birds filled the air.

Rikter found ways to amuse himself while he vigilantly watched the end of the rod, waiting for the tell-tale bob informing him that a fish was nibbling the bait. He sang an old sailors song about a husband leaving his family to find fortune at sea, but he is lost and returns years later to a sweet reunion. He watched the clouds float overhead and drew images from their shapes in his mind, but always he looked for the bobbing on the end of the fishing rod. The end of the rod never moved the entire day.

Rikter slowly became enraged as the hours passed. After three hours he started to wander aimlessly nearby, kicking dirt into the wind. At the hour of two past noon he was kicking loose stones from the fountain and lobbing them at the cobblestone walls outlining the road by the river. When the sun began to dip toward the summit of the mountains he was growling to himself and when the first shadow of late evening fell over the town he had reached a boil.

Rikter stormed into the water up to his knees. With eyes on fire, face red with rage and brow crinkled he screamed loudly at the river. He then sloshed back to the fishing rod, snatched it up, tore the bamboo line loose and tramped back to the shop doorway. He broke the rod over a knee and flung it aside.

Why can't I catch any fish in the river?! his mind yelled. There are fish in the lake, and the river empties into the lake, so why are there no fish here?

Rikter made a fire while he angrily stewed over his failure once again to catch any fish, then plopped onto the mattress and waited for the cold of night to come. He ate what few berries remained, and listened to the rumbling of his stomach while the fire danced in front of him.

After an hour he heard the soft patter of the dragon as she walked to the bridge. In her mouth she held two fresh killed yalat birds. This time, however, she did not look at him but instead continued across the bridge to her home. When another quiet hour had come and gone he decided to sleep and covered himself with the blanket and laid down on the mattress. He closed his eyes and just before the sweet peacefulness of sleep took him he heard the footsteps outside the shop. He sat up and strained against the firelight with tired and defeated eyes.

Through the mist of orange light, he saw the face of the dragon, Kaezanneth, and in her mouth was a four-winged yalat bird. She was able to duck her head and neck through the tight doorway where she placed the bird next to the fire.

She then pulled away and turned to leave.

"You're welcome," she said softly as she began to vanish into the night.

"Wait!" Rikter called and Kaezanneth stopped to look back.

"You don't know how to speak to dragons, do you, or others as well?" she asked.

Rikter was taken aback. "I don't understand," he admitted.

"I'm speaking of laelliwuel," Kaezanneth said.

Rikter furrowed his brow. He didn't know what she meant. "Laelliwuel?"

"It is what humans call etiquette," she said.

"Oh." Rikter grasped what she meant. "I'm sorry. Please wait!"

Kaezanneth turned to face him and sat just outside the doorway. "Yes?"

"Thank you for the bird," Rikter continued.

"I thought you may be hungry for more than berries."

Rikter took the bird and began to pluck it all while keeping an eye on her. "I am, indeed."

Kaezanneth watched him pluck and clean the bird, skewer it on a stick he found in a corner and prop it into the fire. "Is there more you wish to say?"

"Ah, yes. Why can't I catch any fish in the river?" he asked.

Kaezanneth smiled, careful to keep it simple

so she wouldn't frighten him. "Now you're asking the right question, Goober."

Rikter grinned at her.

"There aren't any fish in the river," Kaezanneth said.

"Why?" Rikter asked.

"I like to fish too, but the fish are afraid of me, so they stay in the lake," Kaezanneth told him proudly.

Rikter felt very stupid. Had he asked why there weren't fish in the river instead of boasting that he could catch fish in the river, he wouldn't have wasted three days fishing. In turn he could have saved himself a lot of time.

"I still don't understand. Can you not just catch them in the lake?"

"Yes, but in the lake they have room to avoid me. The river is narrow, so they have no room to swim away," she said.

"Are you good at catching fish? I would think a dragon would be horrible at swimming,"

"Not so, my wings are excellent for swimming, and I am very good at catching fish."

"And catching small animals in the fields, no less," Rikter added.

"Yes, this is true," she agreed.

Rikter turned the bird over in the fire. The aroma coming from it was very pleasant in his nose. He then looked at the dragon.

"Why are you in my valley?" Kaezanneth

asked him.

"I don't know. All I remember is being tossed off my ship and nearly swallowed by a sea monster. When I woke up I was on the shore of the lake," he told her.

"A sea monster? Was it very big?" Kaezanneth asked very excited. She leaned into the shop until her snout was a few feet from his face. She looked like an anxious child.

"Um, yes it was enormous and had four tails."

Kaezanneth tried to rear up with elation and her head hit the ceiling with a thud. Dust rained down on them both.

"Yeningregger! You saw the Worm of Yeningregger!" she stammered and winced with pain.

"That thing has a name!?" Rikter cried.

"Yes it has a name! It is the Worm of Yeningregger, the great calamity of the seas! What a sight it must have been!" Kaezanneth exclaimed.

"That thing almost swallowed me!" Rikter barked.

"But it did not because, here you are!"

"Yes, I am here where I don't want to be!" Rikter screeched. "Would it be rude to eat while we talk?"

"Yes, but I will allow it because I know you're hungry," Kaezanneth said.

Rikter removed the yalat bird from the fire. The skin was a golden brown and dripping with such irresistible succulent juices that he couldn't deny dipping a finger and licking it clean.

"Where do you wish to be?" Kaezanneth asked, becoming more curious and comfortable with him.

"Home."

"Where is home?" she asked.

"Leonora Ander," Rikter answered before taking a small bite from the cooked bird.

"Is that a village?"

"No. It's the ship I serve on and I need to get back to it."

"Why? Don't you like being here?" Kaezanneth asked, a small part of her hoping he would say yes. She had been alone in the valley for so long she couldn't count the years.

"This place is beautiful, but it's not where I want to be," he said, trying not to be disrespectful. He fell silent as his thoughts went to the Leonora Ander, Brice, Captain Jones and the crew. He also wondered and hoped they had survived the storm and the Worm of Yeningregger. If they did make it to safety, did they think him dead after witnessing his fall into the sea?

Rikter swallowed the mouthful of yalat and stared into the flickering fire longingly, missing Brice and the others like they were his family. When he replayed the memories of his time with them, they were in fact family to him. He let out a long sigh.

Kaezanneth quietly watched Rikter, and her heart felt a little heavy at his words. She lowered her head and spoke softly, "You want to be on your Leonora Ander again, don't you?"

Rikter nodded.

"All you need to do is go over the Crescent Mountains that surround Dayle," she explained.

Rikter raised his gaze to her. "Is there a way?"

Kaezanneth thought a moment. There were two ways he could leave. The first involved flying him over the mountains, but she felt in her heart she would not be able to conquer her fear of heights to do so. As much as she wanted to help him to leave, she was beginning to like him and wanted him to stay. She had grown lonely and he was the first person she had talked to in centuries.

The second way out of Dayle was to climb over the lowest part of the Crescent Mountain Range called The Archer's Bow. It was a very distinct length of mountains that was curved downward from two summits in the shape of a bow. If she told him about the latter, he would certainly leave and she would be alone again.

While she wrestled with whether to tell him or not, he finally spoke.

"Can you fly?"

Kaezanneth's head raised and her nostrils

flared. "What is your meaning? Of course I can fly! I am the best flier in Dayle! Why would you ask me such a question?" she boomed.

"I'm sorry. It's just that I haven't seen you fly yet," Rikter said anxiously.

"I will show you someday. Tomorrow! I will show you tomorrow!" Kaezanneth declared.

"Will you fly me over the mountains so I can return to my ship?" Rikter asked hopefully.

Kaezanneth was stunned by his request. Her heart thrummed heavily and her thoughts turned to the night she crashed in the valley. It was a long time ago and she was knocked from the sky by a surge of bluish, crackling light. It was like lighting but a thousand times more brilliant. The bolt struck her down and burned like she had touched the sun. The world spun and everything went dark. She could not see her mother and father or the rest of her Brood-Wing and she could not speak over the thunder to call for their help as she fell from the darkened sky. When she awoke she was in the fields belonging to Arie's father.

Kaezanneth shook her head quickly, again trying to break free of the memory.

"Will you fly me over the mountains, please?" Rikter pleaded with her.

"No. No I cannot. I will not!" she sputtered and backed out of the shop.

"Why not?"

"I will not leave my home!" Kaezanneth

stated firmly.

Rikter stood to face her. A sick feeling inside his belly rose like the tide. "You don't have to take me home, just over the mountain and you can return," he bargained.

Without another word she turned and started to leave.

"I don't believe you are a real dragon! Dragons are supposed to help people, are they not? If you were one you would help me. So, are you a real dragon or not?" Rikter said angrily.

Kaezanneth spun to face him and raised an eyebrow. "What do you mean 'are you a real dragon'? What else would I be? Just look at me!" She spun her back to him, unfurling her wings. They glimmered in the fluttering firelight. "Look at my wings and tell me what other creatures have wings like mine?"

Rikter was stunned by the shimmering colors of her wings and the breadth of their span. Indeed she was impressive.

"And look at my tail!" She shoved her tail in his face and flapped it. "Do I not have the tail of a dragon?"

"I suppose," he said.

"You suppose?" Kaezanneth parroted back excitedly. "What is your meaning? Haven't you ever seen a dragon, before me?"

Rikter shook his head. "No I have never seen a dragon."

Kaezanneth gasped. "How could you have never seen a dragon? We are everywhere!"

"Dragons left the Nine Isles more than three hundred years ago," Rikter told her.

"YOU ARE LYING!" Kaezanneth roared and Rikter fell backward in a fright. "How dare you make such a claim that dragons have gone from the world!"

"It's not a lie!" Rikter exclaimed. "If they didn't leave, then why is it that no one has seen a dragon in such a long time?"

Kaezanneth snorted a small plume of fire in anger that scorched the ceiling. "I cannot answer that, but everything you said before is a lie! Dragons have been in the Nine Isles since the day the world was made! We are eternal, like the earth! I will not help a man-boy who lies! I will not fly you over the mountains, but I will be glad to see you leave! Go to the north and west to the mountains that bow to the horizon! It is there that you might survive your escape from Dayle! Good night, Rikter the Goober! You have two days to leave my valley before I eat you, with or without ketchup!" she growled and stormed off in a rage. In her voice was not only anger, but a sadness she was masking.

Rikter dashed outside to follow her, but she heard his footfalls and suddenly leapt into the air. She spread her wings and with a mighty thrust, soared away, but no higher than a tall tree. The dirt on the road swirled into a giant cloud beneath her and engulfed him.

She barked loudly to him as she glided to her house. "Do not follow me to my house! You are not invited!"

Rikter watched sullenly as Kaezanneth disappeared into over the river. She landed at her home in a brisk run and hurried into the back of the house where she ducked into Arie's room. She grabbed the doll and laid her head on the blankets, then cried until she fell asleep.

11
JOURNEYS, REVELATIONS AND LOSS

ONE

In only three days the Skydancer had crossed the northern plains of Ellamar and began to cross the Southern Horn Sea toward Caledonia.

She had flown one-hundred miles, high above the grassy hills and flatlands. It all quickly passed beneath her hull like a blur since she left Skyvale. Peasants, farmers and travelers on the roads watched in awe of the ship that sailed overhead without water or wind. They pointed, shouted and some were even frightened having never seen an airship before. At the bow of the Skydancer flew seagulls that kept her pace as though she were one of the flock.

When the undulating sea was three-hundred feet below, the ship seemed to pick up speed as if an unseen hand was pushing. In fact, the Skydancer was faster when flying over water and was unmatched by nearly any animal that could fly.

As the ship raced across the sky for the homeland of the elves, Lady Samarra spent her time enjoying the lengthy conversations with Eochus and Thareg about their travels.

Hildegrinnel on the other hand, stayed in her quarters below deck with her nose buried in magical texts and scrolls. When Lady Samarra knocked on her door during the first day of their journey, Hildegrinnel dismissed her saying that she was studying what little was written about the library.

On the third day, when the northern shoreline was shrinking into the horizon behind them, Lady Samarra ventured onto the main deck and made her way to the forecastle. Her armor was replaced with an ox-hide tunic trimmed in fur and layered cloth and leather breeches that were tucked into her long boots. Draped over her shoulders was a crimson fur cloak that she cinched about her person to stave off the chill.

Lady Samarra stopped at the rail to the bowsprit and watched the straight line horizon of the sea. Around her the crew went about their work as she drifted away in her head. The thoughts she had were not on the beauty of the enormity of the vast amount of water beneath the ship, nor was she concerning herself with the mystery of a library unknown to the world. No, she was focused on the circumstances that led her to cross the sea and leave her home.

There was a fire in her heart that was usually reserved for more pleasant things such as morning breakfast with her husband, riding through the countryside on horseback as he pursued her, or learning swordplay from him in the courtyard gardens. After recent events, that fire was now a malevolent entity that consumed her.

If the Divines were kind to her, she would have her revenge and the people of Ellamar would have justice.

Lady Samarra stood there on the deck, as still as stone, and did so even when Thareg quietly appeared at her side.

Off the port side of the Skydancer the sun prepared to kiss the edge of the world under a veiled haze of orange and red hues. The colors reflected off the surface of the sea like an explosion and cast rays streaming across the bow.

"The sunsets at sea are the most beautiful in all the world. Wouldn't you agree, my lady?" Thareg declared softly. When Lady Samarra didn't respond he listed his head toward her. "My lady, are you well?"

Lady Samarra snapped out of her thoughts with a jerk. "Huh, oh, I do apologize, Captain, I was…elsewhere for a moment. You were saying something?" she stuttered.

"I was simply remarking about the beauty of the sunset," he said.

"Oh, yes. Yes, the sunset is quite lovely here. I don't believe I have ever seen one quite like it before," Lady Samarra admitted.

"Forgive me, my lady, but up until this evening you seemed to be enjoying our voyage, but to see you now I wonder if your intentions on this ship are of a personal matter?" Thareg guessed.

"Yes, Captain, I have enjoyed being here. It is a wonderful ship," Lady Samarra began with a tear rolling down a cheek. She wiped it away and continued, "You are correct. I am here for a personal reason of which I will not say."

"I understand, my lady," Thareg said, taking notice of the tear she wiped from her reddened cheek.

"Thank you," she said and flashed him a forced smile.

Eochus quietly walked up to Thareg, as much as a dwarf weighing twenty-stone can, and with his usual charm announced, "Captain, my lady, by my calculations we will arrive at the southern coast of Caledonia in two days, around dawn, as long as our speed holds."

Thareg looked at his first mate. "Thank you Eochus."

"Eochus, what, may I ask, do you mean if our speed holds?" Lady Samarra asked.

"Nothing to be too concerned with," Eochus said. "Occasionally the Skydancer changes speed over water."

"Is that why I feel like we are moving faster than over the land?" Lady Samarra asked.

"Yes, my lady," Thareg answered her.

"Shall I tell her why, captain?" Eochus

asked with a smile stretched across his wide face.

"I don't see any reason not to," Thareg said.

"The spell on the Skydancer grants flight over land with incredible speed, and even faster with water under her, but there are times when the magic flounders. It happens only over water. Most times she is fast, and other times she is a little slow," Eochus said.

"But master Eochus, there is water beneath the hull while we were over the land," Lady Samarra pointed out, confused.

"Yes there is, my lady. The water under Skydancer's hull looks like water, and behaves like water, but water it is not. What you see on the hull is an illusion."

"Why does genuine water affect the magic in the ship?" Lady Samarra asked.

"Because, my lady, water is unaffected by magic," Thareg enlightened her.

"It is like trying to make fish smell good with more fish," Eochus joked.

"Does that not create problems when trying to outrun a storm?"

Thareg replied, "The change is very small, my lady, no matter if the ship decides to go faster or slower."

"The Skydancer is just like a woman, if you ask me, Captain. She never seems to be able to make up her mind."

"That she is. However, over land our speed

is always fifty leagues a day, while over water we've gone as fast as sixty-five."

Eochus grunted his disapproval as he said, "On a good day, perhaps, Captain."

Thareg chuckled at his remark. "Is that all you have to report, Eochus?"

"I certainly wish, but Hildegrinnel has asked that Lady Samarra see her at her earliest convenience," The dwarf said as he gave Lady Samarra a warm smile.

"Understood," Thareg began. "Eochus would you escort the Lady of Ellamar to Hildegrinnel's cabin?"

"Happy to Captain," Eochus chirped.

"Thank you Captain. Mr. Eochus, after you," Lady Samarra said politely and she followed the dwarf below deck. Along the way they passed the five Gray Knights gathered in the common room sitting around a table eating supper. They bolted upright in respect as she entered and sat down as soon as she exited. They arrived outside Hildegrinnel's cabin and knocked.

The door swung open by itself. "Please come in, my lady," Hildegrinnel said.

"Thank you Eochus," Lady Samarra said then stepped inside to find her witch seated by the bed at a tiny desk as her butterflies flitted about. Several books were stacked on it and under the light of a floating candle Hildegrinnel was hunched over a large, old leather bound book. Her staff lingered beside her, balancing itself upright between the desk and bed. The tiny tree's leaves on top of the staff began to turn brown and gold with the coming of autumn.

"Thank you for coming so quickly, my lady," Hildegrinnel thanked her.

Lady Samarra quietly went to the bed and sat beside her. "Hildegrinnel, it was of no consequence. This is a small ship and it would make no sense to prolong my coming."

Hildegrinnel chuckled. "I agree, my lady, it would make no sense."

"Now that I am here, what need have you of me, Hildegrinnel?"

"I will not keep you long, my lady, I have information about the library and something disappointing to tell you before we arrive," Hildegrinnel began then closed the book and turned to face her. "I will be as brief as I can, my lady."

"Being brief is a rare occurrence with you I have noticed."

"Ah, yes of course, then I will continue. The library is somewhat unknown to me and I am confident it is a result of my failing memory. One of my Order, Jinndellihar is his name, told me of a journal he came to possess about the library. The writings tell it is guarded by something that was not meant to protect it," Hildegrinnel said.

"What would that be, exactly?" Eochus

asked. He was still outside the cabin and unintentionally overheard their conversation.

Lady Samarra looked toward the dwarf and grinned. "Yes, Hildegrinnel, and what do you mean by 'not meant to protect it'?"

"Sadly, my lady, that is what my Order could not discover. In the journal Jinndellihar has, the writings only said that the earth, and the very stones in it, would keep anyone out who tried to enter, but there was no reason for such an action given."

"That is about as helpful as a shield made of paper," Eochus said, the sarcasm of his words thick as syrup.

Hildegrinnel snatched her staff, pointed it at the doorway and the cabin door shut tightly in Eochus' face.

"For a witch of a royal court, you lack manners!" Eochus said loudly as he walked away.

Lady Samarra stifled her urge to giggle and asked, "Whatever awaits us at the library, we will face it together. What is the disappointing news you have for me?"

With reluctance, Hildegrinnel continued, "I fear you will not have your revenge. The voice from the sky sent ripples throughout the Nine Isles. My brethren in the Order felt it as I did. There is an otherworldly power present that borders on the divine, and as we all know, mortals do not affect the Divines."

Lady Samarra said nothing as her eyes glared back at the witch.

"My lady, I implore you to turn us back to Ellamar. I will journey to the library myself and seek out the responsible party to Lord Greggory's death. This is a path that I fear would only sadden you more."

Lady Samarra digested her words carefully, and with a look of defiance she said, "If you are correct, and there is a divine power at work, I will not rest until either I strike down the entity responsible, or die in the process." She stood rigidly. "No creature, Divine or mortal will sway me. Good night Hildegrinnel." With those final words she left the room and retired to her own quarters for the night.

TWO

Rikter spent the next two days preparing to traverse the place where the mountains bow to the horizon. The first thing he did was pull a length of thread from the blanket and thread it through a makeshift needle he fashioned from a cotter pin he pulled from a wagon wheel hub. With it he stitched together the blanket in such a way that when he was done he had himself an oddly crafted coat.

The next thing he did was to retrieve the

rope that had tangled him up when he first met Kaezanneth. That was also the day when she chased him into town and pounced on him. After a thorough search of the buildings in town he was fortunate enough to find a rusted pickaxe with a broken wooden handle. He smacked the handle on a rock until it was free and tied the rope to the pickaxe head using a bowline knot. The rope had seen better days, but it was all he had and it was the only one he had found.

Satisfied and rather proud of his ingenuity, he turned his attention to what to take to eat. If he managed to get out of the valley, he had no idea how far it would be to a town so food was a necessity.

The day before he left he journeyed to the lake and caught several fish, which he scaled, cleaned and dried out using a salt rock to cure. With a large palm leaf he wrapped the dried fish in it and stowed it into a bag he made from a piece of burlap.

During all his preparations he kept a vigilant eye for Kaezanneth, but she never appeared. He was certain that she would have at least been spying on him as he hurried about. A few times when he thought she was around he would jerk his head to look but all he would see was either a bird or squirrel venturing about. It was an odd thing, he had thought once or twice, that he should miss her company having only known her for a few days, and only speaking with her for but an hour.

What he most likely was unaware of was that he liked her. She was deceptively generous, as evidenced by the items she had given him such as the blanket, boots and the yalat bird. She had to be compassionate to give those things. Also she could've ripped him to shreds when they first met, but she didn't, so mercy and reasonable thought were apparently hallmarks of her personality. These qualities he had been privileged to witness were all qualities that any number of people looked for in a friend, and he wanted to be hers.

He was saddened by the thought of leaving the valley without her, but the outside world had a strong hold on Rikter. It was so strong that he didn't want to invite the notion of staying in Dayle.

If only she would leave with him.

Rikter's last night was spent alone, bundled in his new coat with a warm, glowing fire. His meal before he fell asleep were the berries he was forced to eat when he couldn't catch any fish in the river. He smiled wide when he thought of how foolish he must have looked to her, trying to fish in a fishless river. Each time he thought of her trotting past him saying he would not catch anything in the river, he chuckled.

Yes, Rikter liked her and even though they had only known each other a few days, to him it felt like she had been his friend for a lifetime.

When morning broke over the eastern ridge of the crescent shaped mountains trapping the valley, Rikter awoke much differently than he had before. He quickly gathered his burlap satchel, the rope and pickaxe. He slung the bag on one shoulder and the makeshift climbing rope and hook on the other then hurried outside.

He crossed the abandoned plaza and the dry fountain where he went over the old wooden bridge for the last time. Far off into the west, at least a day's walk, he took notice of the bow-shaped dip in the western line of mountains. The lowest point of the curve was considerably less tall than the rest of the range. He set off through the fields of tall, golden grass at a brisk pace with hope in his heart.

It took him a couple hours but he eventually emerged from the field where a forest began. Sitting beside a thick oak, as still as one of the trees, was Kaezanneth.

The look on her face was one of heartbreak. She took a few steps toward him and sighed.

"Please don't go. I'm sorry I got angry," she said with her eyes on the ground like a child seeking forgiveness.

For a dragon to apologize was a very rare event.

Rikter's heart fell inside his chest. He had hoped that she would've stayed away. It would have been easier for him to leave without seeing her.

He sighed too. "I have to…um…I don't even know your name, but I have to leave."

"A dragon's name has to be earned," she told him calmly, but told him anyway. "My name is Kaezanneth, second daughter of Kaellaneth."

Rikter smiled at her. "Kaezanneth. That's a beautiful name. I've never heard anything like it."

"Will you stay now that you know my name?" Kaezanneth asked, hope heavy in her voice.

"It isn't that easy. I wish that I wanted to stay here, but I don't belong here," Rikter told her regrettably.

"You can belong here. Just give it some time and you may love it like I do," she pleaded.

"I don't think that will happen. There is only the two of us in this entire valley, am I correct?"

"Yes, but I was here a long time alone and I am very happy here," Kaezanneth declared.

"But I know I can't be happy here. The world on the other side of those mountains is my home. Come with me and maybe you can find out what happened to the other dragons. Don't stay here alone."

"Nothing happened to the other dragons, and I'm not really alone here. I have Arie," said Kaezanneth.

"Your sister?" Rikter asked.

"Yes," Kaezanneth answered quickly.

"Where is she?"

"Home, where she always is," Kaezanneth said.

"I didn't see her there," Rikter told her, referring to the day they first met.

"She was there. You took her from her room."

"The doll?"

Kaezanneth nodded.

Rikter understood her meaning. She treated the doll like it was Arie. Without question she was alone in this large valley.

"Were there other people here at one time?" he asked.

"Yes, there was a lot of people," she said proudly.

"And where did they go?"

Kaezanneth's thoughts went directly to a time when the people of Springwater were alive and thriving. It was a time that she cherished with all her heart. The people of the town were generous and caring. They lived together in harmony, worked together in unity, celebrated together like family and unfortunately they died together. One, by, one.

Kaezanneth whined pitifully then shook her head vigorously, like she was trying to force the memory from her mind. She shut her eyes but tears forced their way through the edges of her lids. She slumped to the ground and covered her face with her feet-hands.

"Kaezanneth, where did they go?" he asked softly.

"No, I don't want to talk about this. Please just stay with me and don't ask me anymore about this," she whined.

Rikter slowly approached and knelt near her. He reached out with a hand and touched her head, gently petting her. Tears were in his eyes as he spoke, "They died didn't they?"

She nodded and the color of her body shimmered until she was a deep blue.

"Are you the one that buried them by the church?"

She nodded again and said in a very hushed tone, "Yes. They got sick. They all got sick and died," her sobs sounded like the cries from a pup for its mother.

Rikter could feel her pain of loss as though it had happened to him.

"Arie and her family died too, didn't they?"

Kaezanneth nodded feebly. "I couldn't help them! I wanted to help but I couldn't!" she cried.

All the memories she had struggled to suppress came crashing down on her like an avalanche. When she heard Rikter say Arie's name she writhed out of his reach and reared up, roaring into the sky like a boom of thunder with her wings outstretched. She slammed into the thick trunk of an oak with a shoulder, splitting the tree with a loud crack. The tree fell over into another tree breaking the braches on one side until it slammed into the earth.

She turned to Rikter who had fallen back at her sudden outburst. Her eyes were swollen with rage and sadness. An orange glow lit up the insides of her nostrils. "NOOOO!"

Rikter tried to scramble to his feet but she lunged and pinned him to the ground. "You are staying here! I won't let you leave me like they left me!" she screamed.

Rikter threw his arms across his face. "I can't, Kaezanneth! I won't!"

"PLEASE!" Kaezanneth begged, her voice shrill and filled with an unlimited sadness.

"No! I don't belong here!" he shouted desperately. "And Arie wouldn't want you to stay here and be sad for eternity! Come with me!"

"I can't leave Arie! Don't you understand? She's my sister and I won't leave her here!" Kaezanneth roared.

Rikter took a deep breath for what he was about to say, and he was certain she might kill him for it.

"ARIE'S DEAD AND SHE ISN'T COMING BACK!" He boomed then rolled into a ball, peeking through the gap in his arms, waiting for her sad rage to kill him.

Instead, he saw her raise onto her hind legs and her mouth opening wide. From the back of her throat an orange and red glow radiated within and her flexible tongue twisted in her mouth, dividing it into two halves. Hot fire rolled out of her gullet like living death and sprayed from her mouth in the shape of a 'v', scorching the earth around Rikter, but not touching him. The fire hissed like a thousand snakes as it roasted the ground with a heat that was unlike anything he had ever felt in his entire life.

When the flames subsided she bolted into the fields, her mighty feet pounding the earth with loud thuds as she galloped away from him. He could still hear her sobs as she ran away. The ground on either side of him was blackened and the grass turned to ash. Remnants of her wrath burned in small spots around him.

Rikter climbed to his feet and looked in the direction she had gone. His heart was beating like a feverish drum and sweat covered his face, but his heart was heavy with what he had to say to her.

He sighed long and waited for an hour to see if she would return, but she did not do so. Dejected, Rikter turned and headed for the mountains that bowed to the horizon.

THREE

The Skydancer soared over the tops of the clouds then swooped beneath the fluffy layers as the ship raced hundreds of feet above Caledonia. It was almost as beautiful as Ellamar.

There were rolling hills covered in lush tall grasses that were still green and swayed in the early autumn winds. To the north, at the edge of the expanse, was a great forest that went on for miles in all directions and a wide river that cut a swath through it all. At the center of the mass of trees was a wide clearing and a crystalline lake whose surface was as blue as the sky. Beyond the forest and lake, towering nearly into the clouds, were the Crooked Mountains, called so because it was two ranges that ran into each other from the east and west. The craggy peaks traveled north until they converged and continued more than half the length of Caledonia.

The library that Hildegrinnel was so adamant about needing to get in to was somewhere near the lake, but to approach without caution was unwise.

Standing stoically on the quarterdeck beside his first mate, Thareg Longtooth commanded the Skydancer. The main deck was alive with activity as the small crew prepared the fire-orb cannons and the forward ballistae, a large crossbow that fires eight-foot long, thick arrows.

Lady Samarra and Hildegrinnel took their places on the quarterdeck with Thareg and Eochus. The lady of Ellamar donned her battle armor and flowing red sash along with her late husband's long-sword, Knaythrandire, on her hip. Gripped tightly in her left hand was a small circular shield forged just for her. Fierce determination was written in her glare as the anticipation enveloped her.

Hildegrinnel stood beside Lady Samarra, brandishing her magical staff. However, unlike Lady Samarra, the witch was apprehensive about the entire voyage after she had conversed with the other mages in her order. She didn't relish the idea of seeking out who was responsible for Lord Greggory's death anymore. Her concern wasn't for herself, but for Lady Samarra's safety. In spite of this, she was bound by her word to serve and no matter if the path they were on led to their demise, she would serve without question.

Occupying the main deck of the Skydancer were the five Gray Knights that had accompanied the Lady Samarra and Hildegrinnel. Like their Lady of Ellamar, they too were eager to fight. Each had an assortment of lethal weaponry from swords to battleaxes and each also had a tall shield on an arm.

The Skydancer began to descend when it neared the clearing, so close to the treetops that the wake from the hull scared the birds from their roosts.

"Careful, Eochus," Thareg warned his first mate. "Take us in very slow."

"Do you really believe the witch, about the

library being guarded by the earth and the very stones in it?" Eochus asked.

"I do not ask that you believe me, Mr. Eochus, just that you take caution," Hildegrinnel said to the dwarf.

"And I would take caution if I knew what exactly we needed to take caution from."

Thareg chuckled, then said, "Regardless of what is guarding this library, I offer a thought, Eochus. Would you want to be ambushed, or ambush those who would ambush?"

Eochus cocked his head in thought. "Your logic is as solid as stone, Captain. Slowing our approach." He then pulled a lever near the helm and the Skydancer slowed considerably.

They leisurely coasted just above the trees into the clearing and over the river. A short distance away, near the north western edge of the lake, was the gleam of white stone in the sunlight. The field that lay between them was covered is rocky outcroppings in all manner of shapes and sizes that zigzagged the ground. The closer they came, the more unnerved everyone felt.

The gleaming stone soon took the shape of a rectangular foundation, and on top of it were two rows of grooved pillars on the east and west edges. At the center was a grayish monolith eight feet tall and on the surface was a carving of a woman in a flowing toga. At the southern end of the structure were two large boulders, covered in moss and vines that were buried halfway into the ground.

"Listen," Lady Samarra uttered and everyone hushed.

The air was completely absent of sound.

"I don't hear anything," Eochus said.

"Neither do I, my lady," Thareg admitted. Compared to everyone aboard the Skydancer his hearing was by far the best.

"Exactly, Captain. There are no sounds. Not from birds, or crickets and even the wind," Lady Samarra told them.

"Most curious," Hildegrinnel muttered. "This is highly irregular."

"I agree," said Thareg. "Ready the cannons and ballistae," he told the third mate on the main deck, keeping his voice tempered in the event he was overheard. The gun- crews on the gun deck, one deck below, went to work priming the cannons and setting the ballistae.

"I don't like this," admitted Eochus as the Skydancer reached the middle of the rocky field.

"Eochus, set us onto the lake and we will disembark from there," Thareg ordered.

"Aye Captain," Eochus said as he turned the ship toward the lake.

The ground below them began to rumble. It was very subtle at first, then it rose like an incoming tide. The grass in the field swayed and the rocky outcroppings trembled.

Everyone on the Skydancer fell silent and

froze. The tension was thick as mud. Heads turned and the Gray Knights went to the rails to look below. The remainder of the crew became anxious and murmurs floated between them of what the sound was and why the ground shook.

"Calm yourselves!" Thareg called out. He felt their anxiety.

"Something bad is about to happen, isn't it?" Eochus asked Hildegrinnel who nodded at him.

The two half-buried boulders ahead of the Skydancer shifted after a millennia of slumber. The earth around them cracked and crumbled as the huge stones wriggled more and more. The outcropping of rock nearby cleaved through the shallow earth, moving to the twin boulders near the library as if they were alive. The thick vines snapped as the enormity of stone violently twisted. As it rose, more earth parted revealing that there was more to the boulders still under the ground. Dirt exploded as a fierce rocky hand burst free and slammed onto the ground, then another erupted into the daylight, and another and still another.

The two boulders moved like any creature of flesh would and began to dig into the rich soil as if trying to free themselves. Soon the two hunks of stone had split the ground enough to allow their legs to move. The living rocks hurriedly flung fistfuls of earth and clay in an effort to climb out of their natural prison until they stood before the

Skydancer and her crew. Each boulder proved to be the body of a faceless creature that had mighty arms and powerful legs, all of stone.

"Of the earth!" Eochus chortled. "How poetic!"

"What are they?" Lady Samarra asked fearfully.

"They are stone golems, my lady," said Hildegrinnel.

"Turn us broadside, Eochus!" Thareg shouted. "Port gunners! Two hundred feet! Fire!" he shouted to the third officer who relayed the order to the gunners below.

The port gunners adjusted the cannons and lit the fuses. A second later the booms of cannon fire filled their ears as thin shelled, iron orbs rocketed from the barrels and sailed at the two giants of stone. An orb struck the body of one and exploded in a brilliance of fire. He giant teetered but did not fall. When the smoke cleared the result was a small crack in the stone. The second stone monster was struck as well and like its brother, it suffered with only a crack along one side.

The stunned faces of the gunners screamed to the third officer, "No damage to the enemy!"

The stone monstrosities each reached for the piles of stones that were part of the outcroppings. They scooped the writhing rocks into their hands.

"What are they doing, Captain?" Lady Samarra asked.

Thareg shook his head. "I am not entirely certain, my lady!"

"They are about to perform their duty, captain!" said Hildegrinnel.

"Eochus, full speed! Hard to starboard!" Thareg commanded.

Just as the Skydancer swung her nose away, the stone golems hurled their handfuls of living rock. The ship barely escaped being struck and raced east before circling around the golems. As the living rocks sailed harmlessly by, everyone aboard thought they heard chattering, high pitch voices.

Were the rocks actually alive?

The golems again scooped up more stones and threw them at the Skydancer as she raced around the clearing overhead. The ship easily dodged their attack. The cannons fired another barrage of fire-orbs that boomed like claps of thunder against the hard skin of the stone golems. They scooped more handfuls from their piles and slung them at the ship. The stones scattered across the Skydancer's path as she swooped around the to the north.

"They're going to hit us!" screamed a crewman.

Hildegrinnel waved her staff and just as in Skyvale, the butterflies swarmed from within the small tree and became a million in their numbers. They formed a crescent shape and the rocks merely bounced off harmlessly. That is, all but one. It slipped through and struck the deck with a loud smack. Before anyone could inspect it, the rock sprouted arms and legs and stood. It was but two feet tall and carried a short sword made of stone and had a jagged mouth full of craggy teeth, but no eyes.

"What is that creepy little thing?" cried Eochus.

The little stone man suddenly dashed about the deck swinging the little sword feverishly at the Gray Knights. The stone blade only made sparks fly off their steel plate armor. The knights drew their own swords and attacked the small warrior only to find that he was very nimble. He ducked, slid and dove from every effort to strike him. All the while it laughed in a shrill, cackling sort of way. When one of the Gray Knights did strike a blow his sword clanged against the stone skin, leaving only a deep gouge, and sent the little stone man skittering across the deck.

The stone warrior quickly returned to his onslaught. He leapt at one of the knights and the tip of his little stone sword found a spot between the chest plate and shoulder to stab. The Gray Knight groaned and fell to the deck, dead.

Giggling with demented delight, the stone man went after another knight like the first. In mid leap the head of a war-hammer, wielded by another Gray Knight, shattered the small attacker into a pile of gravel.

"They are some kind of imp!" the Gray Knight who had killed it declared loudly.

"Swords are useless!" said another. "Use the war-hammers!"

Another volley of the stone imps rained into Skydancer's path. Hildegrinnel again cast her spell but she was too late. Two dozen stone imps made it to the main deck and wasted no time in sprouting limbs and attacking the crew. Tiny little stone swords slashed as they dashed about from person to person. What their dull blades did not cut, the pointed end could stab. Their maniacal screeching laughter made their onslaught much more confusing as the Gray Knights and some of the crew fought back. Bits of stone littered the deck as one by one stone imps were smashed in the battle. Three of the imps stabbed several crewmen and then rushed to attack another Gray Knight.

Several stone imps then bounded up to the quarter deck and lunged at Lady Samarra. She dispatched the vicious little minions with several swings of her small war-hammer. To her surprise she enjoyed smashing them. It was a liberating experience.

Thareg took the helm from Eochus. "You're needed in battle my friend. Take up Earthshaker and show them to their end!"

Eochus' large toothed grin spoke volumes

about how exited he was to be included in the fight. "As you wish, Captain!" He bolted away to the main deck and into the officer's cabin beneath Skydancer's helm. There he found his five-foot tall war-hammer named Earthshaker. The head of the weapon was the size of a wine barrel and made from an extremely heavy and hard metal called gillendrinithiel. Carved into it were the Dwarven runes of enchantment. It gave the hammer the ability to echo the vibrations of anything it struck, and amplify them back.

Eochus grabbed the stout wooden handle and stormed back outside.

Four stone imps were chasing after a crewman when he emerged and with one swing of Earthshaker, Eochus pulverized them into ash. The hammer head rang out like the gong of a loud bell.

"I love this hammer!" he boomed with laughter and set to work destroying each one that crossed his path. "Come to Eochus you little devils, and meet your end!"

Thareg piloted Skydancer in a continuous circle around the stone golems as the cannons fired shot after shot into them with only minimal results. He was able to avoid several of the stone imp groups that the golems kept tossing. He watched as the piles of rocks at their feet were being fed by the outcroppings in the field.

"We need to stop the imps from being

replenished," he said to himself. "Gunners! Change your aim to the rock veins in the field!" he roared to his third officer.

The cannons soon found their new target and unleashed a relentless amount of fire on the field. The rocky outcroppings seemed to cry out in pain as they were decimated under the Skydancer's onslaught.

The stone golems turned to the field to witness the end of their little stony warriors and then let loose their anger at the ship in the sky. The both tore into the earth at their feet and unearthed boulders almost as large as themselves. They lifted and hurled them into the air.

The first one sailed by the bow, narrowly missing the ship. The second large rock grazed the keel on the port side and sent the Skydancer listing steeply. Everyone on deck lost their footing. A Gray Knight and four crewmen unfortunately tumbled right over the rail and fell to the ground a hundred feet below. Their screams were the last sounds they made.

Lady Samarra and Hildegrinnel began to slide but the witch used her staff to summon a magical vine that tied them to the mizzenmast behind the captain.

Thareg clung tightly to the helm and dug his feet claws into the wooden deck. He looked to find Eochus slam Earthshaker into the deck where it became wedged and anchored him in place. The remaining stone imps bounced across the deck and fell over the side.

"This is the most fun I've had in a very long time!" Eochus declared. Just then Earthshaker jerked loose and they both fell victim to gravity. As they began their plunge over the side of the ship, Thareg appeared from out of a cloud of cannon smoke, swinging on a footrope. He reached out to Eochus and their hands grasped one another.

Lady Samarra and Hildegrinnel breathed a sigh of relief when Thareg caught Eochus, and with such grandiose style. It was almost surreal.

"You are amazing, Captain Longtooth!" Lady Samarra complimented.

"My friend, you are heavier than you appear!" Thareg remarked of his first mate as they swung freely.

"Gravity is a real downer, Captain, and if you haven't noticed, I am carrying a seven stone battle hammer!" Eochus hissed.

"I did notice that." With a smile, Thareg tossed Eochus onto the bowsprit during their upswing. Upon his return he felt the rope vibrate and looked up. A stone imp was on the rope line a dozen feet away and chewing it with his gritty teeth. Just when he realized the danger he was in, the rope snapped.

Captain Thareg Longtooth, the most unique captain of any lifetime in the Nine Isles, plunged earthward to his end, disappearing into a cloud of cannon smoke.

Eochus, Lady Samarra and Hildegrinnel cried out helplessly as they watched him fall.

With a heavy heart Eochus summoned what was left of his resolve and climbed along the bowsprit as the ship finally righted itself. He then hurried back to the helm, tears filling his eyes and anger in his heart.

Lady Samarra wanted to say something to Eochus but the time was not now. She had only know Thareg a few days, but even she felt the loss.

The ship suddenly shuddered with the force of an earthquake as it sustained a direct hit to the port side by a boulder. The wooden hull snapped inward as easily as poking a hole in tissue paper where the huge stone became lodged. The added weight dragged the ship closer to the ground.

Eochus fastened Earthshaker to the rail and took the helm. His face was etched with hatred over the death of his friend. "Those devils want to fight, then we will give them one! Hold on to something!" he told Lady Samarra and Hildegrinnel.

"What are you going to do?" Lady Samarra asked him.

He looked to her, and despite his anguish, he grinned devilishly, "Something that may be fun, or lead to our death!"

12
SISTERS OF DESTINY…
ONE MORE TIME

Kaezanneth cried all the way back to her house. The memories that Rikter had forced her to confront were now free and she couldn't lock them away any longer. All she could see in her mind's eye were the faces of the towns people as they became ill one by one, including Arie and her parents.

Everyone got sick…except her. Then everyone died…except her.

She couldn't help them. She was powerless to help them, and she was forced to watch them all die. With all the power that the dragons had at their disposal, the one power they never had was to heal the sick.

Kaezanneth loved everyone in Dayle, and Arie even more so. Her attachment to them all was binding. These were people that took her in and made her feel welcome. They had never seen a dragon before because Dayle was cut off from the world, so when they saw her she expected them to be frightened. Instead they met her with friendly curiosity and compassion.

Arie was the first to find her, and before long they were as close as sisters. Then, after sixteen wonderful years, it was all taken away as suddenly as the night she lost her dragon kin.

The pain of losing them all tormented her again and again every time she slept, and so she locked it away. Anytime the past threatened to overtake her she simply shook her head vigorously as if waking herself from a dream.

Kaezanneth rushed into the house through the rear wall and quickly plopped her head onto the blankets. She clutched Arie's doll to her chest and sobbed woefully.

After a few minutes a sound outside her window made her look up and a strange woman's form walked by the window. She sneered and rose up.

Who was that!? Is someone else in my valley now!? she shouted inside her head. I don't care who it is, they must leave just like Rikter the Goober!

Kaezanneth's inner rage consumed her and she hurried outside to confront the interloper. She galloped around the house and slid to a halt. Standing in the front of the house was a woman almost as tall as her wearing a long, black gown with a red sash tied about the waist. Her hair was the color of gold and very short. Her eyes were strange in the daylight, like two shimmering pools of mercury.

"Greetings, Kaezanneth, second daughter of Kaellaneth, Queen of the Dragons," the woman said most properly. Her voice was soft and very kind. "My name is Angellevere, the Divine of Courage, and I am a Sister of Destiny."

Kaezanneth's eyes went cold and narrowed. She readied herself to pounce by lowering her head and raising her hind quarters. Her wingtips pointed skyward as she twitched her scales, making a rustling sound. She was trying to scare the intruder, but instead it amused the Divine.

"I do not care who you are or how well you greet me! You are in my valley and I don't want visitors! Ever again!" Kaezanneth growled.

Angellevere grinned. "I know what transpired between you and the Waycross boy, great Kaezanneth."

"How do you know my name, or Rikter's?" Kaezanneth demanded.

"I know everything about everyone in the Nine Isles, my dear, and I know you need to leave with Rikter."

"Why?"

"Because he is your friend and you are his," Angellevere said.

"No! No! If he was my friend he would have stayed here with me and Arie!" Kaezanneth replied.

"Where is Arie, Kaezanneth?"

Kaezanneth was confused by her question. If

she knew everything about everyone, then why was she asking where Arie was?

"Don't you know?" Kaezanneth asked Angellevere. "You just said you know everything about everyone."

"Of course I do," Angellevere said and she seemed to glide toward the dragon. "But do you?"

"What are you doing? Stay away!" Kaezanneth demanded as she backed away.

In the blink of an eye Angellevere was within reach of the dragon and touched where her heart was. "She's in here, isn't she, Kaezanneth?"

Kaezanneth reared back, stumbled on her own feet and fell. Where Angellevere touched her a warm feeling surged throughout her body. The feeling was familiar. "Arie? I can feel Arie!" she gasped.

"Yes you can, because she is in your heart. She never left you when she died," Angellevere said to her.

"She stayed with me?" Kaezanneth said as tears wet her face.

"Yes, and she's been trying to tell you something ever since Rikter arrived. You just have to listen," Angellevere said and smiled warmly. "You have suffered more than a creature should. It's time to leave."

Kaezanneth looked away to the grave stones where Arie and her parents were buried and a voice spoke to her in her mind.

"Kae!"

Kaezanneth whirled around when she heard her name being called. Her eyes darted, searching desperately for the human girl who had become her sister. It was Arie's voice. "Arie!" she called loudly.

"Kae, why are you still in Dayle?"

"Arie, where are you?"

"I'm with you, Kae.

"I miss you Arie," Kaezanneth sobbed.

"I miss you too, Kae, but you are sad here. You are dying here and my heart is breaking for you."

"What do I do, Arie? Help me," Kaezanneth begged.

"Go with Rikter. Rejoin the world. Be the amazing Kae that made my life so wonderful, and share that happiness outside Dayle."

"I can't leave here. It's our home."

"It was, but now Dayle is a only memory of a peaceful people who lived life together. Our memory lives in you now, and you must carry on for us. Can you do that, Kae?"

"I can't do it, Arie."

"Yes you can, Kae. I believe in you."

Kaezanneth was crying as she nodded. If Arie believed in her, then there wasn't anything she couldn't do.

"I'll go with Rikter, but I will never forget you for as long as I live," She said to her sister.

"I will never forget you, Kae. I love you."

"I love you too, Arie," Kaezanneth said and then, like a lit candle snuffed out by a strong breeze, Arie was gone. She looked over to where Angellevere was. "I think I can go now. I just need to get something first."

"Do you mean this?" Angellevere asked and lifted her hand. A gentle mist hovered over her palm and coalesced into the shape of a doll. It was Arie's doll.

Kaezanneth nodded.

Angellevere went to Kaezanneth. "Are you sure you don't want to leave it here? Where you are going, you might lose it."

"I might, but I am very good at keeping track of it," Kaezanneth boasted. She wiped her face dry with the back of her forearm. "Besides, I can't sleep without it."

"Very well. I will give you a gift, Kaezanneth." Angellevere took her sash and ripped a piece from it. The cloth shimmered like yellow fire. "This sash is unbreakable by mortal means. With it you will never be apart from Arie's doll and no harm will come to it while you wear it." She then tied the doll to the ribbon and made a loop. She placed the doll around Kaezanneth's neck.

Kaezanneth smiled at Angellevere. "Thank you," she said looking down at Arie's doll. When she looked up, the Divine of Courage was gone.

Without another thought, she went to Arie's stone and kissed it one last time, then turned and ran toward the bowing mountains. She leapt into the midday sky, thrust open her wings and in several powerful beats, soared away from her home.

TWO

"Where is the boy now, Gwendelor?" Caroleythia asked anxiously.

"He's about to climb the Archer's Bow in Dayle," Gwendelor told her sister.

"Is the dragon with him?"

"No, she is not. That is odd. I thought Angellevere was going to convince her to go with him," Gwendelor said before looking to Amandonia. "Did she talk to the dragon?"

"Yes she spoke to the dragon," Amandonia answered. She was resting on her couch by the hearth.

"Do they make it over the mountains?" Caroleythia asked. She was very worried for Rikter.

Gwendelor added, "Yes, Amandonia, does the boy make it over the mountains?"

Amandonia did not answer them. She looked at each sister with blank, calm expression, then yawned.

"Sister, please tell us what happens to the boy!" Caroleythia begged.

"I will not say," Amandonia said.

Gwendelor's jaw fell open. "Why would you stay quiet about this?"

'Yes, why would you remain quiet?" Caroleythia pleaded.

"It is simple, really, sisters. If I tell you the fate of every decision everyone makes, you would become as bored as I am," she told them.

After some quiet thought, Gwendelor reluctantly nodded and looked at Caroleythien. "She is not wrong." Caroleythia sighed, wrung her hands nervously and went to the window. As she passed their ice crystal sphere, she noticed a black rat sitting on the table. Its fur was smooth like silk and it had a tiny, twitchy pink nose.

Caroleythia stopped to observe it, then remembered where she saw a rat like this one. "Uh oh. Sisters, is this rat who I think it is?"

Gwendelor rushed over to the crystal table. "Did you say rat?" She saw the rat exploring the crystal.

"Yes I did. Oh dear, please tell me this isn't Rosey," Caroleythia stuttered.

Amandonia casually made her way over. Upon seeing the rat, she gave a nod. "Yes. That is Rosey."

"Right you are, niece," said a voice none of them had heard in a thousand years.

When they turned they found their aunt sitting on their dressing chair beside the wardrobe. She was short for a Divine. Her eyes were like two liquid emeralds ringed in auburn. Her hair was twisted into long tendrils that draped down her back. She also was very athletic. Almost as much as the Divine of Hunters, who was the strongest Divine in the heavens.

"Aunt Tahnazuu! How good to see you after all these years!" said Caroleythia excitedly. Her chest was about to explode.

"I am sure of that," Tahnazuu said tersely. She turned her glare on Gwendelor. "And have you anything to say, niece?"

"I do, but Father always said if I haven't anything pleasant to say…"

"Enough. What about you dear Amandonia?" Tahnazuu asked.

"Greetings dear Aunt Tahnazuu? You look well," Amandonia said calmly.

"What brings you here, Aunt?" Caroleythia asked politely, veiling her distress with niceties.

"I am pleased you asked. I was visiting my brother, your father, and he told me something I found rather odd."

"I can't imagine what that could be," Gwendelor said.

"I can, dear nieces. He told me that Yeningregger had been set loose upon the Nine Isles," said Tahnazuu.

"That cannot be," said Caroleythia. Her face turned pale immediately.

"Oh, but it did happen. I looked into it and there he was, creating chaos throughout the world on the open sea...sixteen years too soon!" Tahnazuu growled.

"I saw this weeks ago," said Amandonia and she went back to her couch to lay down and watch.

"You did?" Gwendelor balked.

"Oh yes, sister." Amandonia smiled back.

"Oh dear," stuttered Caroleythia.

"Ladies, your attention!" Tahnazuu commanded. "Does anyone here know why Yeningregger only awakens every twenty-five years?" she asked reaching down to allow Rosey to climb her arm and take her place on a shoulder.

"Because if he didn't sleep the mortals wouldn't be able to sail ever again," Gwendelor answered.

"Yes. Now can you tell me why you woke him?" Tahnazuu asked.

"Didn't our father tell you?" asked Gwendelor.

"Yes he did, but I am giving you the chance to tell me your version of this catastrophe."

Gwendelor hesitated to answer and Amandonia watched with disinterest. Caroleythia, on the other hand, was pacing nervously.

"Who woke Yeningregger?"

"I did, Aunt Tahnazuu," Gwendelor

admitted.

Tahnazuu sighed heavily and went to the window. She turned her head to Rosey and gave her pet a kiss on the nose. "Why would you do this, Gwendelor? What purpose would you have to awaken that vile serpent?"

"She had a good reason," Amandonia added.

"Yes I did," Gwendelor said.

Tahnazuu went to Gwendelor and gazed into her eyes deeply. "Please tell me, because when you summoned him you offset the balance for those mortals who live below us."

"It was necessary," Gwendelor said.

"Necessary? For what reason would you have to awaken that horrible beast?" Tahnazuu implored.

"We needed him to get the boy off the ship and to the Valley of Dayle," Caroleythia told her.

"What boy?" Tahnazuu asked, rather confused at this point.

"Your son, Aunt Tahnazuu. Our cousin," Gwendelor told her regrettably.

"My, my son?" Tahnazuu stammered.

"Yes, dear Aunt," Caroleythia said.

Tahnazuu felt a wave of realization run up her spine and she went cold with worry. She knew exactly who they meant. Her heart thrummed excitedly, just as it should when a mother knows their son may be in danger. She stuttered his name from her lips, "Rikter?"

13
WHAT GOES UP...

ONE

The Skydancer limped in an arc over the trees as it began to spiral to the earth. The extra weight of the boulder lodged in the port side was dragging her down, fast. Eochus struggled with the helm, despite his great strength, as he aimed the bow at one of the stone golems. He was bound and determined to execute at least one of them before the day was done.

"Are you going to do what I think you're going to do, Mr. Eochus?" Lady Samarra asked, her eyes wide with terror.

"I'm afraid so, my lady, unless you have a better idea," Eochus said.

"I do, but it would not kill either of those things!" she replied.

A boulder smashed the crow's nest as it soared overhead. The wreckage smacked into the main deck with a maddening crash and ripped a hole to the deck below. The gunners below were forced to abandon the guns when their path to the gunpowder stores was blocked. They emerged through the wreckage and joined Eochus topside.

"The gun-deck is destroyed, Mr. Eochus!"

one of the gunners said. "We cannot reach the powder and lost four when we took that last hit!"

"A sad day for us all, but we've no time to mourn! Brace yourselves! We're going to ram those monsters!" Eochus growled.

"My lady, our dwarf friend may have just lost his grip on sanity," Hildegrinnel joked at the most inopportune moment. Lady Samarra just looked at her with disbelief.

Another boulder spun wildly as it sailed by the ship, grazing the hull with a deafening scraping sound.

When the bow was lined up with the closest golem, Eochus shoved the throttle lever to the full speed position. The golems shook their fists at them, as if daring the ship to come closer, and their roars of defiance rumbled like thunder.

"Shout all you like, stone abominations!" Eochus cried as the Skydancer closed the distance between them. The ship picked up more speed as it dove like a hungry eagle after a rabbit. Everyone on the deck grabbed rails and tied loose ropes, still attached to riggings, around their waists as the golem Eochus had targeted filled their view.

"This is for the captain!" Eochus screamed.

A moment later, everyone screamed.

TWO

The majestic walls of rock that were part of the Archer's Bow in the Crescent Mountains surrounding Dayle were deceptively smooth from the valley floor. Up close they were sharp, craggy and a mess of crannies and nooks. Rising for three thousand feet into the sky, they were still the shortest compared to the other peaks. The two summits that made the bow loomed another six-hundred feet higher and curved inward like a pair of vultures eyeing a meal.

Kaezanneth clung tightly to the rugged wall of rock as she expertly clawed her way upward. She had very little trouble climbing. Dragons were built to not only fly, but climb as well. She had followed Rikter's scent, and he smelled foul and was easy to locate, making her tracking skills almost unnecessary.

However, the higher up the Archer's Bow she climbed, the colder it became until the snow flurries blinded her and the wind bit harshly without remorse. What made matters worse was that she lost sight of him in the swirling mass of snow, forcing her to slow down. Even so she was willing to fight nature to join Rikter on his journey over the mountains.

She was also fighting her fear of heights as she clawed her way higher and higher. When she tried to look down she shut her eyes so tight her face hurt.

One day, she thought, I'm going to fly as high as I want to!

She tried to look down again but her neck joined her eyes and refused to allow her to look.

"So now my neck and my eyes are against me?" she said to herself. Just then she remembered how Rikter had a habit of talking to himself, and she had just done it herself.

Great! she thought. I'm talking to myself like him! Does that mean I'm going to be clumsy like him, or a goober, too? I hope not!

She leapt another dozen feet and sank her claws into the rough stone, then did so again and again. If she didn't think, or try to look down all the time, she was sure she could avoid panicking and catch up with Rikter very quickly. Feeling a surge of renewed determination, she continued her leaping ascent to find her new friend.

THREE

The Skydancer's forward keel plowed into the stone golem's body, slamming it into the earth with a bone shaking thud, where it broke into several pieces. The ship then cleaved a huge ditch forty feet long in the ground, scattering large chunks of dirt across the field.

The forward ballistae took a tremendous shock from the crash and triggered the firing mechanism. The bolt rocketed from the ship and shattered the second stone golem's knee causing the monster to fall. The massive girth of the golem shook the ground and it let out a shrill cry, as if in pain.

The lower decks were obliterated from the crash. The main mast broke mid-beam and collapsed onto Eochus, pinning him under the bulk. Twisted ropes, smashed rigging and ripped sails buried the dwarf from sight.

Lady Samarra was thrown forward and flipped onto the main deck where she fell through a hole in the floor. She landed in the gun-deck atop a pile of wreckage, and would have been injured had it not been for her armor.

Hildegrinnel was struck on the head by a plank and rendered unconscious as she was thrown across the quarterdeck. She was caught by several crewman. The ship finally came to rest on its port side just a dozen feet from the injured stone golem.

Eochus tried to move but discovered that he was trapped. When he tried to lift the beam across his chest he found it to be too heavy to lift.

The stone golem began to crawl toward the wrecked hulk that was once the Skydancer, slamming the ground with one hand while pushing forward with its one good leg. Grumbling sounds came from within the body of the stone beast. It slammed a hand into the gunwale on the port side, tearing into the once beautiful wood as easily as crushing a tin can.

Lady Samarra was first to recover and get to her feet. Her head spun like it was on a turntable as she climbed through the hole back onto the main deck. She quickly looked about. She saw the stone golem near the bow, smashing and clawing while it pulled itself along the length of the ship. The cracking and snapping of wood was like the sound of bones breaking and sent a ripple of urgency up her spine. A gasp stole her voice and rendered her speechless.

What was driving these calamitous creatures to destroy them?

Lady Samarra rushed to the where Eochus had been to find the crewman clearing the debris.

"Where is Eochus?" she asked them hurriedly. Hildegrinnel came to her side. On the witch's forehead was a nasty lump where she had been hit.

"He is under all that you see, my lady," Hildegrinnel said.

"Then let's make haste and free him!" she ordered as she grabbed the heavy sail and dragged it from the pile.

The crewman hurriedly joined her and soon cleared enough of the debris to find Eochus still trying to lift the mast. When he saw them he smiled as though nothing was wrong.

"Hello, ladies and gentlemen! How did we

do?" Eochus greeted them. "Did we send those things back to the ground?"

"We've no time for jokes, Eochus!" Lady Samarra said urgently. "Quickly men, get him free!"

"Yes my lady!" said one of the crewmen and they scrambled to lift the mast. With the three of them they were still unable to free the dwarf even when using a plank as a lever.

The stone golem had torn his way through most of the ship and was now midway to where they stood. It raised a hand and punched a hole through the deck. Wood splintered like toothpicks with a sickening crack. The monster then growled at them.

"Hildegrinnel is there a spell you can use to get him out?" Lady Samarra asked desperately.

"No, my lady. My magic is unable to levitate objects. I can however slow the beast," she said stepping toward the monster. She raised her staff and chanted a spell in a unrecognizable language. Thick vines sprang from the ground and grabbed the golem by a leg and an arm and tugged strongly against the incredible strength of the stone beast. The golem clutched the main mast that was pinning Eochus with inhuman defiance.

"You must hurry! I cannot keep him back for long!" Hildegrinnel cried.

Lady Samarra went to help the men when someone large limped up to her and the crewmen and startled them all.

Holding a bleeding wound on the left side of his abdomen was Captain Longtooth. He touched Lady Samarra's arm and she looked up at him, frozen with astonishment. "I will free him. Get everyone clear," he said.

"Captain!" Lady Samarra gasped. "You're, you're…"

"No time. Go," he said.

Lady Samarra ordered the men to get away from the ship as she went to Hildegrinnel. "The captain is alive! We need to get clear! He's going to free Eochus!"

Hildegrinnel was pleased Thareg had survived his fall. She turned and followed Lady Samarra. They clambered over wreckage and rigging until they were on solid ground. Ahead of them the crewmen had gathered near some trees.

Thareg stepped where Eochus could see him.

"You ruined my ship, Eochus. I expected you to take better care of her," he joked.

"Captain! You're alive!" Eochus exclaimed. "You must've landed on your feet again, I see."

"Quite correct. Hold yourself, my friend, this may hurt." Thareg said. He lifted Earthshaker over his head. This was the only way to free him.

Eochus smiled. "Always wanted to see if I'd survive my own war-hammer."

"Easy Eochus, I'm going to strike this blasted mast," Thareg said and he swung

Earthshaker with everything he had. The hammer slammed into the wooden mast and it exploded into a thousand splinters. The impact rattled the dwarf but did not kill him.

Just as the golem reached the quarterdeck and swung a powerful hand to squash them, Thareg snatched Eochus by a collar and leapt clear. The golem's hand obliterated the quarterdeck as it slammed a fist repeatedly into the wreckage.

Thareg and Eochus tumbled on the ground nearby. The rough landing sapped what strength Thareg had left and he lay still. Eochus recovered and went directly to his captain and friend.

"Captain, are you okay?" Eochus asked in a panic.

"I'll be fine, my friend. Don't mind me. We still have a problem," he said pointing at the golem. It had already managed to tear through the ship and was hobbling toward them on one leg and a knee.

Eochus looked to the golem, then back at Thareg. "I'll be but a moment, Captain," he said and went to collect Earthshaker. He took up his weapon and rushed toward the stone monster.

The stone golem raised a hand to crush him, but Eochus swung the hammer and caught the broadside of the body with a powerful blow. The stone golem teetered backward as a chunk of it broke off and fell to the ground.

Eochus swung again and the impact sent the monster reeling. He then ran at the beast and slammed Earthshaker into its knee.

"You're not going to knee-d this anymore!" Eochus quipped as the golem's leg shattered like glass. The golem fell onto its back where it was as useless as an overturned turtle.

Eochus then delivered the final blow, to the spot he had already struck, with such force that the golem broke in two. The golem groaned one last time then fell silent.

Lady Samarra and the crewmen cheered the destruction of the stone golem from where they had gathered then ran to attend Thareg.

Winded and sore, Eochus returned to Thareg and dropped to his knees. He looked at his friend. "How are you feeling, Captain?"

Thareg sighed. "I feel like I fell a hundred feet off my ship," he chuckled.

Hildegrinnel and Lady Samarra smiled at him.

"Is he going to be okay, Hildegrinnel?" Lady Samarra asked.

Hildegrinnel whispered at her butterflies and one landed on Thareg's wound, then its wings turned color to a soft emerald.

"He will heal in a few days, if he abstains from any fall from a great height."

Thareg gave her a wry grin. "I will do what I can, Hildegrinnel."

"Captain, it is a great relief you are alive," Lady Samarra said.

"Thank you, my lady. Now I implore you both to see to the library before any further interruptions," Thareg told them. "Those things meant to destroy us without knowing our intentions, and I would greatly appreciate a reason why it cost me my ship."

"I agree, captain, and I will get you an answer," Hildegrinnel said with a turn, and she started toward the slab of stone that was supposed to be a library.

Lady Samarra hesitated a moment.

"I will be fine, my lady. Go. There are more important matters to attend to than me," Thareg told her.

"As you wish, Captain," Lady Samarra said then rushed to join Hildegrinnel, eager to learn why Greggory was taken from her.

FOUR

Dragons are a wonderful and remarkable creature. They have little trouble adapting, are masters of flight, exceptional climbers, and are skilled fishers. Their scales can endure intolerable heat, and even deflect the blow from swords and are nearly impenetrable to arrows. However, under extreme cold temperatures, the most hardened dragon suddenly becomes a shivering, helpless child.

Kaezanneth was no exception when it came to the freezing cold. She had reached the summit of the lowest point in the Archer's Bow, and found that the snow was as deep as her chest. The flurries fell without respite and buried the mountaintops. She frantically searched for Rikter along the edge but could find no trace of him.

Was he still climbing? How did she reach the top before him? What if he fell? A feeling of dread overwhelmed her. She had to find him.

Her body shivered as the icy winds penetrated every crevice of her scales. Every muscle ached from the cold until the pain became like fire, burning every fiber her body. Her lids became heavy and all she wanted to do was lay down to rest, but she knew if she did she might not wake up…ever. Fighting her natural weakness of the cold, she pressed on.

Snow whirled and twirled in the twisting winds as she continued to look for Rikter. Then she heard a clang that was just loud enough to pierce the howling winds. It must have been the crudely made grappling hook he had fashioned together smacking the frozen rocks of the sheer wall of stone.

She rushed toward the sound and through the deluge she saw Rikter climbing up the rope. He was nearly to the top when the knot around the pickaxe slipped loose.

Rikter was now a passenger of gravity and fell from sight.

Kaezanneth's heart jumped into her throat and she roared his name loudly. She bolted to the edge, shoving the snow aside with her powerful arms and leapt off the mountain. Her fear of heights tried to strangle her resolve, but the thought of Rikter in distress was stronger than the fear. Her heart raced as she rocketed along the cliff face toward Rikter. She was going faster than she had ever gone in her life. The tip of her snout started to form an ice cap over her nose as she picked up more and more speed. She could hear Rikter screaming as he tumbled through the air.

Then he disappeared behind a rock butte in the cliff face. With no time to turn, Kaezanneth drew in a deep breath, the heat inside her belly burned like a raging inferno and she suddenly spit a ball of fire at the outcropping of rock. The stone exploded in a ball of fire and smoke just before she tore through the plume. Shattered rock rained from the sky as she emerged from the smoke only to discover another outcropping separating her from Rikter.

Kaezanneth was carrying too much speed to be able to spit another fireball. She tucked her head and rammed into the second rock outcropping with her shoulder. The stone shattered much like the first but sent her spinning out of control. She wanted to cry out but her mouth refused to obey. She struggled against the spin and caught a glimpse of Rikter. He was so close now that if she weren't spinning wildly she could've touched him.

She cried out. "RIKTER!"

Rikter looked in her direction and his face went from terror to bewilderment faster than they were falling. "Kaezanneth!?"

Kaezanneth's heart felt complete now that he had seen her. She twisted her body and using her tail like a rudder she was able to angle her fall until she was facing him just an arms length away. Rikter reached out desperately and grabbed at Kaezanneth's neck, clinging to her like a lost child. He could feel the warmth from her and it was like a blanket of reassurance.

"You came back!" Rikter shouted.

"Of course I did! You're my friend!" Kaezanneth admitted, then she hugged him like she used to hug Arie. When she looked down at Rikter she could also see the ground a thousand feet below them. It seemed to spin before her eyes and before she knew what was happening, her fear had returned. The sky around her blackened into night and she was no longer falling. Ahead of her now was the wing of dragons being led by her father, Gaellenkarth and her mother Kaellaneth. Around her were dozens of dragons of all colors and sizes and she knew them all.

Was this a dream or was her time in Dayle a

dream?

Then she heard Rikter's voice in the clouds that had gathered. Lightning streaked across the sky and thunder shattered the night. Suddenly the wind whirled before them all and became a torrent of chaos. The dragons cried out as they were devoured one by one by the storm. Just as it was about to swallow her a bolt of lightning struck her and she tumbled from the sky. She screamed and cried for help but none came and she was so very afraid that she shut her eyes and waited for the earth to meet her.

Rikter's voice rang in her head. "Kaezanneth open your eyes! You need to fly or we'll die!"

"I can't fly! I can't! Please don't make me!" Kaezanneth begged. The air rushed by so fast and cut their skin like tiny knives.

"Kaezanneth, you can fly! I know you can!" Rikter shouted. They had just fallen below the snowline and the air started to get warmer.

"No! I can't!" She stammered with her eyes tightly shut. The poor dragon was trembling with fear after reliving the night she fell to Dayle.

Rikter climbed around onto Kaezanneth's back and wrapped his arms around her neck then leaned toward her ear. "You can do this! You're a dragon and dragons fly!"

"Well that may be but not this dragon!"

"I saw you fly!"

"I'm afraid of heights!" She cried.

"WHAT!? What kind of dragon is afraid of heights!?" Rikter exclaimed.

"How would you know!? I'm the first dragon you've ever met!? We could all be afraid of heights!" She barked back at him.

"That's the dumbest thing I've ever heard!" Rikter yelled. "You have wings and you are meant to fly over the clouds not under them!"

"Says who!?" Kaezanneth yelled back.

The ground came at them even faster. A hundred feet from the treetops Rikter started kicking her shoulders where her wings began.

"That hurts! What are you doing?" She demanded.

"I'm trying to make you open your wings!" He said and kicked again.

"Stop it!" She growled.

"Then fly and I will!" He kicked her again This time she twitched and her wings sprang open. The air filled them like the sails on a ship and they soared into the sky. In only a few moments they were so high that Rikter could see the lands beyond the mountains.

"We're dead! Oh we're dead aren't we?" Cried Kaezanneth. She hadn't opened her eyes yet and was blubbering. "Oh woe is me! We're dead!"

"We're not dead, Kaezanneth! You did it! You're flying! It's the most amazing feeling in the world!" Rikter shouted joyfully.

"No we're not! You're just saying that to make me feel better! We're dead and we have to spend eternity in the afterlife together! It seems a fitting punishment for you but not for me! What did I do to deserve to spend forever with a goober!"

"Open your eyes, Kaezanneth! We are not dead!" Rikter told her. "Believe me like I believe in you!"

Kaezanneth cracked an eyelid just enough to look. Stretching in all directions around her was the valley of Dayle, and everything beyond. To the west was a great expanse of grasslands and rivers of such beauty that filled her with awe. The north was no less impressive as beyond a winding river was a thriving forest that disappeared into the horizon. To the east and south she could see the blue-green waters of the Skyvale Fjord, and the Sea of Ellamar. The midday sunlight shimmered on the dancing surface of the water.

Tears welled up in her eyes as she looked down upon her adopted home. "I'm flying!" She banked north and dipped her nose, picked up more speed and then she barrel-rolled before spiraling into a nose dive with Rikter clinging to her very tightly. She then curved upward and performed a loop. She hooted her excitement to the very sky.

Rikter smiled and let out a cry of elation for her.

Then the wind blasted them from everywhere without any warning and converged to a point in their path. The air whirled and whirled as it grew and grew.

"What is that?" Rikter asked.

"I don't know and we are not staying to find out! Hold tight!" Kaezanneth said before she banked and tried to put some distance between them and it. In her mind she was afraid of the disturbance. It reminded her of the night she came to Dayle. She hoped that whatever it was it wasn't the same thing that separated her from her parents.

The cyclone of air spun faster and faster and began to pull on the dragon and her friend. The faster Kaezanneth flapped her wings, the more it pulled at them.

"We're not moving!" Rikter shouted.

"I know!" Kaezanneth said. She was starting to tire out. It had been three hundred years since she had flown so high and fast that her wings were out of shape. She felt her lungs begging for air and her muscles aching for relief, but there would be none.

"What's wrong, Kaezanneth? We're going backward!" Rikter shouted over the noise.

"I'm tired! I can't keep this up!" She gasped, then finally succumbed to the wind. They both screamed and were swallowed by the strange vortex. As quickly as the phenomena had appeared, it vanished into the air and was gone.

14
THE FIRST KING

ONE

Lady Samarra and Hildegrinnel cautiously approached the granite monolith at the center of the stone floor of the Athenaeum of the Ancients.

The pillars bordering the edges towered over the women like rigid guardians. There was an eerie calm hovering over the entire humble structure that neither could explain. The carving of the woman in the monolith at the center was very intricate and extremely lifelike as it stared quietly toward the southern horizon. In the shadow of the surrounding trees there should've been autumn leaves somewhere on the stone slab they were crossing. Instead the floor was clean and smooth. Not a speck of dirt or leaves were present.

Lady Samarra drew her husband's sword, Knaythrandire, but Hildegrinnel placed a hand on the hilt. "Take care, my lady, but we will not need your husband's sword. There is no fight here."

"How can you be so sure, Hildegrinnel?"

"Look at the floor around us. There is no dirt or leaves on it. This place is protected by magic," Hildegrinnel told her with a reassuring smile.

"Is that magic responsible for those behemoths and those horrible little imps that tried to cut us down?" Lady Samarra asked.

"No. I believe the magic keeping the leaves and earth out is meant to protect this place, but the magic that spawned those things is darker. Remember what I told you from Jinndellihar's journal. The golems and their minions are preventing entry, but the magic around the Athenaeum allowed us to enter. Someone does not want the knowledge here to be learned, that is the reason for those monsters that nearly destroyed us," Hildegrinnel said.

"For what purpose?" Lady Samarra asked.

"I am not sure, but I do know that you will not need your weapon here, my lady."

Lady Samarra sheathed the sword and followed her, but said, "If this is the library, where are the books?"

Hildegrinnel shook her head. "I am not sure. If only I could remember this place."

They continued until the monolith was upon them. The lady in the stone stared blindly over their heads. Her likeness was very detailed. Her hair was long and straight, and the clothing chiseled on her was very much like what the Divines wore. In one hand she held a quill and the other was a scroll. Other than those details there was nothing else of interest.

The longer Hildegrinnel examined the statue

the more familiar it felt, but still her mind was unable to piece it all together. Had she been here before today? If so how long had it been since she was here?

"What do we do now?" Lady Samarra asked.

Hildegrinnel shrugged.

"Welcome," said a chorus of voices.

Lady Samarra drew her sword and spun around, while Hildegrinnel only looked up to the statue.

"My lady, you need not panic. The voices came from the statue," Hildegrinnel said calmly, pointing to the sculpture. As sure as the day brings the sun, the woman of marble and granite had indeed spoke and looked down at them.

"Welcome Lady Samarra Baylen of Ellamar. Greetings to you as well Hildegrinnel of the Order of Six," the blank-eyed statue said. Her voice was like a thousand beautiful voices speaking in harmony. It was melodious.

"How-how do you know us?" Lady Samarra asked, hesitant to sheath Knaythrandire.

"I am the keeper of all knowledge in this world. The day you were born was the day I became the keeper of all you do," said the stone lady.

"Is this place the Athenaeum of the Ancients?" Hildegrinnel asked.

"No, this place is not," answered the statue.

Lady Samarra groaned her displeasure,

"We've come to the wrong place, Hildegrinnel!"

"No, Lady Samarra of Ellamar, you have not," began the statue. "If the Athenaeum is what you seek, then you have found it. I am the Athenaeum."

"This is most interesting," Hildegrinnel gasped.

"You are the library?" Lady Samarra asked. She sheathed Knaythrandire again and stepped closer to the carved woman. It watched her with an expressionless face.

"Yes I am. What do you wish of me, Lady Samarra Baylen?"

Lady Samarra looked to Hildegrinnel, who gestured for her proceed. "My husband, Greggory, was taken from me. The assassin that killed my beloved was turned to ash by something that came from the sky. It was a voice that spoke of the true king. I want the name that voice belongs to!"

"I shall answer your question. The true king is the first king of the Nine Isles, and is the voice you heard in the skies above Skyvale," the Athenaeum told her.

Lady Samarra furrowed a brow without understanding. "How can that be? The first king of the Nine Isles was King Jaissen of Elsemere, was he not? That was nearly two thousand years ago!"

"It was one-thousand nine-hundred and fifty-seven years ago, Lady Baylen, but the voice above Skyvale was not the voice of Richard Jaissen. He was not the first king. He was the second king," the Athenaeum corrected her.

"I am at a loss," Lady Samarra admitted.

"As am I," Hildegrinnel agreed.

"The first king was the gargoyle king, Bahraam of Revelstoke. He ruled the Nine Isles for four thousand years."

Lady Samarra gasped. "I don't understand. How can a dead king from thousands of years ago, order the death of my husband!? And why would he want him dead!?"

"Your husband was to be the next king of the Nine Isles," the Athenaeum said.

"I still don't understand," Lady Samarra admitted. Exhaustion had taken her patience. "Just tell me everything that concerns my husband's death!"

"As you wish. Bahraam the gargoyle king was imprisoned prior to the second reign, by the Order of Six. The spell required someone to be the life-force of the seal that keeps him locked away. Each king of the Nine Isles regenerates the seal and keeps Bahraam imprisoned. When the last king passed on in the year sixteen twenty-six of the second reign, no new king was chosen, and the magic holding Bahraam began to fade. Your husband was killed because he was to be the next king. With him gone there is no hope of keeping Bahraam in his prison. He now will return and retake the world unless a new king is crowned."

"I do not remember any of this," Hildegrinnel said.

"Your memory is failing you, Hildegrinnel, as a result of your extreme old age," the Athenaeum said.

"Is there any way to kill Bahraam?" Lady Samarra asked.

"No. He cannot be killed by mortal hands."

"No! No! I will not be denied vengeance in my husband's name!" Lady Samarra growled and paced angrily.

"If you wish to take from Bahraam as he took from you, my lady, then you must prevent his arrival," Hildegrinnel told her.

"How? There needs to be a king of the Nine Isles!" Lady Samarra snapped.

"Then we must find this king. How do we accomplish this?" Hildegrinnel asked the Athenaeum.

"To find a king for the Nine Isles, you must have a dragon," the Athenaeum said.

The two women looked at each other with confusion. As far as they knew, the dragons vanished from the world and the last mention of them was over three hundred years ago.

"The Dragons are gone, are they not?" Lady Samarra surmised.

"No, Lady Baylen, they are not. There is one dragon left in the Nine Isles," the Athenaeum told her.

"Where is it?" Lady Samarra demanded, her tone dire. "Is it close to us?"

"The dragon is in Ellamar," said the Athenaeum, "But she is leaving with a young man named Rikter Waycross for the land of East Hold."

Lady Samarra threw her hands up in frustration. "How are we to reach them? The Skydancer is destroyed!"

"There is still hope, my lady, we will have to be patient. There is a village called Torrey to the east. We can secure transportation from there to Leiffdell Port where we can book passage aboard ship to East Hold," Hildegrinnel explained.

"No Hildegrinnel, that will not do! Time is short! We need to see this dragon now and ask for it to help us!" Lady Samarra exclaimed, desperation thick in her tone. "Can you not use your magic to take us to her?"

"No, my lady. No spell I know can transport us over such a great distance." Hildegrinnel said regrettably.

Lady Samarra felt her chances of some sort of revenge slipping away. The thought of failure twisted her insides.

"There is a spell that will bring the dragon here," offered the Athenaeum.

Lady Samarra went to the statue with

hopeful eyes. "There is!? You must tell us the spell! Please!"

"As you wish. Hildegrinnel, repeat these words, 'With wings of leather, from an age older than time, a new king's brow, a crown must find. I beseech the creatures, whose wisdom is true, this evil we cannot, defeat without you."

Hildegrinnel felt a familiarity once more, as if she had said those words a long time ago. "Athenaeum, have I said these words before today?"

"Yes, Hildegrinnel."

"When?" the old witch asked.

"You said them when you wrote the spell," the Athenaeum told her.

Lady Samarra grimaced at Hildegrinnel. "You wrote the spell that summons a dragon?"

Hildegrinnel shrugged. "I suppose I did, my lady. Now if you would pardon me, I will bring forth our only hope of stopping Bahraam," she said, and raising her staff, she spoke the words.

At first nothing happened. Then the world fell silent in their ears. Behind them a faint sound, like a whisper, made them turn. A wisp of bluish smoke seemed to grow from a point as small as a coin only a few feet away. It was suspended in the air as it grew, then twisted into a tendril and began spinning. A strong wind whipped around them that smelled of grassy fields and the sea. Without warning it suddenly opened a hole in the world and a large black, winged creature tumbled out of it, followed by a teenage boy wearing a tattered, patchwork coat.

As quickly as the hole appeared, it vanished.

TWO

The creature recovered quickly and like a confused animal it surveyed its new environment. Seeing Hildegrinnel and Lady Samarra, it lowered its body like it was about to pounce. The wingtips pointed skyward and the scales on its body flashed different colors and vibrated, making a scratchy sound. The mouth of the creature sneered at the end of a hard muzzle, displaying sharp teeth. Two short horns twisted skyward from both sides of its head above where ears should have been. The creature looked around. Upon seeing the boy, the it rushed over, placing itself between him and them. It was protecting the boy who had not moved but was moaning.

Lady Samarra held up her hands as her heart raced frantically. Hildegrinnel was very amused and smiled warmly at the creature, as though she had seen its kind before today.

"Who are you!?" the creature roared. "Where are we!?"

"She talks!" Lady Samarra uttered in disbelief.

"Of course I talk! What of it?" the creature said. "Now answer me! Who are you and where is this place? Did you bring us here!?"

"Calm yourself, please," Hildegrinnel said softly. "We will not harm you."

"Harm us? That is very funny little woman-human!" the creature guffawed.

Lady Samarra chuckled, "Please. Listen to us. My name is Lady Samarra Baylen. I'm from Ellamar, and this is Hildegrinnel."

"Just explain yourselves!" the creature demanded.

"Are you a dragon?" Lady Samarra asked.

"That's a stupid question! Yes, I am a dragon! Why does everyone keep asking me that? Now, stop asking me these questions and start telling me what is the meaning of all this?"

"We summoned a dragon to us, and here you are," Hildegrinnel began. "You are in a land called Caledonia."

"I know of Caledonia."

Hildegrinnel smiled warmly. "We needed to speak with you, but our ship is destroyed and our only means for reaching you was to bring you here."

"Why do you need to speak with me?" the dragon asked.

"It is very simple, really, my dear," said Hildegrinnel as she explained. "We need you to choose a new ruler of the Nine Isles. What is your name, if I may ask?"

The dragon lowered her wings and raised her head. "My name is Kaezanneth, daughter of Kaellaneth."

"And the boy? Who is he?" Hildegrinnel asked.

"He is my friend, Rikter," Kaezanneth told her. "As for choosing a king, I am not the dragon you seek. You need my father. He was next to do so."

"You are incorrect, Kaezanneth, daughter of Kaellaneth the Queen of the Dragons," said the Athenaeum.

Kaezanneth hissed threateningly at the voice she had heard but could find no owner, "Who said that!?"

"Calm yourself, Kaezanneth!" Lady Samarra implored. "What you heard was the Athenaeum." She pointed to the statue as it smiled at her.

"This has been a very strange day, and I want to go home now," Kaezanneth said, cowering at the sight of the living stone face watching her.

"You must not go, or ignore us," Hildegrinnel pleaded. "If you do not chose a king, Bahraam will return and take the world for his own."

Kaezanneth froze where she stood upon hearing her words. She knew the name Bahraam from the stories her mother and father told her. He had done horrible things to all the races of the Nine Isles for thousands of years. The skies were always dark with his evil magic, the waters in the rivers were like poison, the plants withered and famine was rampant. Hordes of stone minions made in his image carried out his cruel orders. They burned villages, took food from the starving, and destroyed any who resisted by means of war. Humans, elves, and all half-humans suffered as slaves to him and his ilk. That is, all but the dwarves. The dwarves bowed to the gargoyle king willingly and offered no resistance. Bahraam favored their kind for their ability to mine and forge, and he used them to create his armies and feed his treasury.

If these people were telling the truth, and as far as she could tell they were, then she had a duty to seek out a new king. It was her father that had instilled that deep sense of duty in her. He would tell her that a dragon is bound by truth, morality, and compassion. She sighed and looked at the Athenaeum.

"I will listen to you. I cannot allow Bahraam to return," she said. "But as I said before, I am not the Steward of Kings."

"You are the steward, Kaezanneth. You have the mark upon you," the Athenaeum explained.

"My hatchling-mark?" Kaezanneth lifted a

wing and saw the birthmark, shaped like two rings locked together, marring the leathery membrane. "I thought it was from my hatching."

"No, Kaezanneth. It is the mark of the steward."

"But my father did not have this mark."

"He did have the mark. All stewards bare it," the Athenaeum told her.

"Not so," challenged Kaezanneth. "My father's wing held no shape such as this."

"Alas, he did. The mark is never in the same place on each steward. If you think upon it, you may remember he had a mark on his face," the Athenaeum said.

Kaezanneth struggled hard as she searched her mind, and in a flash she saw her father's face. Behind his right eye, she saw it, two darkened rings overlapping, as if joined. She thought it had been the roughness of his scales that made the image.

Just then Rikter sat up. His head hurt like he had been upside down for too long. He looked around and was just as befuddled as Kaezanneth had been only moments ago.

"Kaezanneth, did I miss anything important?" he asked.

"We are in Caledonia," she told him.

Upon hearing that he perked up. "That's amazing! We were just in Ellamar! Did you know you could fly that fast?"

"She didn't fly here, young man, you were both summoned here with a spell," Lady Samarra said.

"Who are you? Why did you bring us here?" Rikter asked.

"We summoned Kaezanneth and you arrived with her," Lady Samarra explained.

"Yeah, so what is the rest of the story?" Rikter asked impatiently.

"They want me to choose the next king of the Nine Isles," Kaezanneth told him. "Are you okay?" He nodded to her. This made her happy.

"Why do you have to pick a king? Why can't we just leave now?" he asked.

"I can't just leave, Rikter. I have a duty to this world."

"So, you will undertake this task?" Hildegrinnel asked.

Kaezanneth nodded to her. "I will."

"I don't understand," Rikter said to her.

"I am the Steward of Kings. I have the mark as such." She showed him the mark under her wing. "I have to do this or your world, my world, will be destroyed."

Rikter felt a sinking sensation in the pit of his stomach. "What are you telling me, Kaezanneth?"

"I can take you to Ironshire, but I cannot stay," she said.

"Um, I-I guess that would be okay."

"But I would much rather you come along with me than return to your ship," she admitted, hopeful that he would agree.

"You don't need me for that, Kaezanneth. I'm just a sailor, not an adventurer," he said with a grin.

"I do not care what you are, only that you are my friend and I would like for you to go with me," Kaezanneth said to him.

Rikter shook his head. He wanted to nod and agree, but his home was pulling at him. "I can't, Kaezanneth. I have to get back to my ship. My friends most likely think me dead."

Kaezanneth lowered her head sadly, and she looked to Lady Samarra and Hildegrinnel. "I will miss you, Rikter." She took a couple of steps, then the air grumbled like an angry bear.

All eyes looked to the sky. Dark, rough clouds coalesced from nowhere and consumed the sun from the ground. The mass formed a ring in the sky, churning as it did above Skyvale and a voice made the very air they were breathing tremble.

"So, Hildegrinnel, you think you have found the Steward of Kings."

Rikter felt a fear he had never known before and he moved closer to Kaezanneth. "Who is that?" he whispered to her.

"That is Bahraam, the First King of the Nine Isles," she said to him in a hushed tone.

"Yes, Kaezanneth, the last of the dragons, I am Bahraam, the true king of the Nine Isles."

Kaezanneth too was afraid, but stood bravely against that fear, and shouted at the sky, "You will not be the king on this world! I will stop you!"

Bahraam's laugh was like thunder, *"Brave words from a child! Your quest to find a king will prove to be a failure. I have ensured that there are none worthy to be king with the death of the Lord of Ellamar."*

"I am Lady Samarra Baylen of Ellamar, and I will destroy you with my husband's sword for what you have done to me and my people!" shouted an enraged Lady Samarra as she shook Knaythrandire at the sky. Her face was twisted with anger.

"The Lady of Ellamar. I did not expect you to be the seeker of vengeance. You are brave, but very stupid. Your threat means nothing to me."

"Then let my threat mean something!" Kaezanneth roared. "I will seek out a king no matter where they may be! From a farmer to a lord, or merchant to beggar, I will find them no matter how long it takes! I will search every corner of this world and use every year of my life to ensure that you stay in your prison! We dragons are the true immortals and I have nothing to do but seek out your end!"

There was a long moment where the

gargoyle king said nothing.

"Very well, dragon, you have forced my hand. I would have liked to watch as you fail in your search, but I see now that you are more determined than I anticipated. None of you shall leave this place. I will end your lives now. Let this place be your graves."

"Hey, don't threaten my dragon you big jerk!" Rikter shouted toward the sky. "You hear me up there!"

"That is not very wise, Rikter," Kaezanneth warned.

"I don't care! Nobody threatens my friends!"

The ring of clouds suddenly burst into flames, glowing with a heat like the sun. From the center of the fire a column of white hot light streaked down on them. The sound was like a hundred-thousand hooves beating the earth. It struck the magical barrier protecting the Athenaeum and sprayed droplets of fire like rain.

The ground shook and knocked them from their feet.

"My barrier will not hold long," said the Athenaeum. "I must tell you how to crown a new king."

"Then make haste before it's too late!" Lady Samarra suggested desperately.

"You must place the new king on the seal in the Tower of Light. At midday, when the sun is highest, the new king must bathe in the fire of the steward," the Athenaeum told them.

"What does that mean? Bathe the king in the fire of the steward?" Lady Samarra asked.

"The dragon must breathe fire onto the new king, my lady," said the Athenaeum.

"Wouldn't that kill the new king?"

"No, my lady, it will not," the Athenaeum answered.

Rikter cowered beside Kaezanneth. "I really don't want to go with you on your quest."

"I know and I understand. I wish you would go with me. I don't want to do this without you," Kaezanneth said.

Rikter grinned at her. "I said I didn't want to go, not that I wouldn't. If this Bahraam returns, what good will it do me to return to my ship and sail, if there is no sea to sail upon?"

"So you will go with me?" Kaezanneth asked, her spirits lifting at his words.

He nodded to her, "I will."

The barrier began to weaken considerably, then just as the magic was vaporized by the fire, Hildegrinnel drove her staff into ground and shouted, "Elitherandere!"

The butterflies surged from her staff and engulfed them all, but it was not quite enough. The fire pulverized the Athenaeum monolith and a fierce explosion decimated it and the floor leaving a crater many feet into the earth. The shield of butterflies shattered like glass and sent Lady Samarra, Hildegrinnel, Rikter and Kaezanneth tumbling like leaves in the wind.

Kaezanneth bounded to her feet and rushed to help Rikter. "Are you okay?"

He was okay but dazed. "I really do not like this Bahraam."

"Neither do I," said Kaezanneth. "Stay here." She went to launch herself skyward but Rikter dove onto her back. "What are you doing?"

"I'm going with you!" he shouted excitedly.

"I could very well die today, Rikter!" she told him.

"Not alone, you won't!" he said, regretting his words immediately. How could he let her go alone, after she saved his life when he fell from the Archer's Bow? No, if she was going to face her death, then he was going to go with her, and die at her side.

Together they leapt into the air and soared directly at the ring of fire. Another bolt flashed past them toward Hildegrinnel and Lady Samarra as they were struggling to their feet. The witch cast her spell of protection again and her winged friends took the brunt of the blast.

Kaezanneth spat a tremendous fireball into the column of fire. The blazing tower of destruction fizzled out rather pathetically. The sky rumbled and Bahraam spoke once more.

"Little dragon, you are nothing more to me

than a nuisance!"

As Kaezanneth and Rikter soared ever closer to the ring, a final deluge of Bahraam's madness tried to destroy them. Kaezanneth let fly an explosive plume of fire that cut a path through the beam but she could not hold it long. When her fire went out they were consumed. Rikter and Kaezanneth had expected to burn but they did not. Bahraam's fire warped around them as if they were in an indestructible bubble. The fire suddenly vanished into nothing like fading smoke.

"Arrgh! What magic is this? What deviousness is this that can resist my power? You are the steward, dragon, but that would not protect you from me. The boy however, he is something else…"

Bahraam's voice trembled as though he was fearful of something, then it was gone. The ring of fire seemed to dissolve with the wind and the angry black clouds parted allowing the sun to again warm the ground.

Kaezanneth and Rikter hovered in the sky upon her beating wings, staring blankly at the sky as it cleared, without so much as a burn from fire that blanketed them moments ago. Why had they not been vaporized by the tower of fire? How did they escape unhurt?

And what did Bahraam mean when he said 'the boy is something else'?

THREE

Kaezanneth and Rikter returned to Hildegrinnel and Lady Samarra, and helped them to their feet. The place where the Athenaeum had been, was a pit of blackened earth and fractured stone. The blast from Bahraam should have turned them all to ash, but Hildegrinnel's spell prevented that much, but could not save the Athenaeum.

Eochus, Thareg and the remaining crewmen soon joined them and carried Lady Samarra and Hildegrinnel back to where they had made a temporary camp. The women had suffered some bruises and scrapes, but were otherwise well.

After introducing Rikter and Kaezanneth to Eochus and Thareg and the crew, they soon sat around a warm fire as the evening approached.

Thareg, Eochus and the crew had many questions about what the women had learned. They also were witness to the ferocity of Bahraam and had many questions about the dead gargoyle king. Nothing in their travels could compare to what had happened there.

"Can the Skydancer be salvaged?" Lady Samarra asked Thareg.

"It can. Eochus is very resourceful. We can be airworthy in a few weeks," Thareg said.

"That is too long. I have to help Kaezanneth

find the new king and put an end to Bahraam!" Lady Samarra declared boisterously.

"I believe, my lady, that the task of finding a new king falls upon the dragon, and she has the final word on how she will proceed."

"But…" Lady Samarra began.

"May I say something, please?" Kaezanneth asked from where she and Rikter were sitting across from them. "With all due respect to the Lady Samarra, I would prefer to seek out the new king with Rikter."

"Isn't he returning to Ironshire?" Lady Samarra asked.

"I was, ma'am, but I can't turn my back on my friend, or this world," Rikter said as he looked at Kaezanneth.

"That is very brave of you, young Rikter, but this is a matter for the Regents of the Nine Isles, not a child."

As Rikter was about to rebuke her remark about him being a child, Kaezanneth nudged him in the side and gave him a look that told him to think better of it.

"I believe that this threat you have uncovered, my lady, is not just a dilemma for the Regents, but for all the people in the Nine Isles," Thareg offered wisely. "I think that everyone here would agree with me."

Lady Samarra glanced at each face around the fire, and each agreed with what Thareg had said with a nod.

"What do you suggest?" Lady Samarra asked.

"I suggest nothing, my lady. I am but a sailor of the skies," admitted Thareg.

"Hildegrinnel?" Lady Samarra asked of her witch, who had proven to be her most trusted friend and advisor on this journey.

"My lady, I will offer this. Rikter and Kaezanneth will journey forth to find a king, while Thareg and Eochus repair the ship. You are needed in Ellamar to assist your son, for he knows nothing that has transpired here, and if the boy and dragon fail, Ellamar needs to be prepared for war. As for myself, it would be prudent that I attempt to restore the Athenaeum to learn the location of the Tower of Light. Without the location to perform the spell, it will not matter if Kaezanneth and Rikter find a suitable king. Are we all in agreement?" Hildegrinnel proposed.

Each person, and the only dragon, gave the matter some thought, then in turn they agreed.

Kaezanneth spoke first her suggestion. "Rikter and I will journey to Ironshire first. He will no doubt want to find his ship and friends before our search for a king."

"I would like that. Thank you," he said to his dragon friend.

"Understood," began Lady Samarra. She then said to Rikter, "But find your ship quickly, young man, and do not waste a moment afterward. The fate of this world hangs on the both of you finding a new king."

"Yes, my lady," said Kaezanneth.

Rikter nodded to Lady Samarra.

"Where do we start our search?" Kaezanneth asked Rikter.

"In the capitol of East Hold," he answered.

"And where is that?" Kaezanneth asked.

"Ironshire."

Kaezanneth's anticipation began to rise. "That's rather ironic! We're already going there!"

Everyone chuckled politely and smiled at the dragon's innocent humor.

"When do we leave?" asked Kaezanneth.

15
THE BETRAYER

ONE

Night fell over the world, creeping along and eating the daylight like a hungry animal would do to its prey. With the darkness came the chill of autumn, and while Captain Longtooth, Eochus, Lady Samarra, and the crew huddled around the warmth of the campfire, Rikter and Kaezanneth sat together nearby, just on the edge of the firelight. They had only known their new allies for a day, and even though they had a common threat to face, they weren't ready just yet to join their camaraderie. One thing they did know, however, these people were an enemy of Bahraam, and that knowledge gave solace to the duo.

It was during this lull in the evening that Hildegrinnel quietly slipped away. Her motive was not nefarious, nor would she ever be, but she needed privacy to do what she must. Her order needed to know what had happened the other day if they were to be ready when the time came to crown a new king. If what the Athenaeum said was true, then the order would be required to heed the call and aid in the fight.

The elderly witch made her way through the

camp and numerous supply crates and barrels, to her tent where she sat on a stool. In front of her was a rickety table containing an assortment of tiny bottles and vials, each filled with an ingredient either liquid or powder. She leaned her staff against the canvas wall and shuddered. A witch or wizard's staff was bound to the user, which meant separation was painful if done so for too long.

She reached over the table to a cloth covering an object that she could not lift, but she could drag it and she did so. Removing the cloth revealed a many faceted crystal that reflected different colors on each face. With gentle fingers she traced a pattern and recited a spell.

"With great distance between us, our words we cannot share, grant our ears the power, to hear what's on the air, gather our small voices, from corners far and wide, and let me hear my brethren, across the great divide."

The world around Hildegrinnel ground to a halt as soon as she had cast the spell. The moth flittering against the top of her tent hung in the air, the wings frozen in time as tiny flecks of dust shrouded it in a tiny cloud. The flame burning the candle wick had been flickering in the autumn breeze when she began the spell, but now it too was motionless, in a petrified state. She looked over a shoulder at her companions gathered around the fire, still as stone statues in the middle of whatever conversation they had been engaged in.

Satisfied that the magic had worked, she turned her attention back to the crystal. Within each facet of the gem were the faces of the Order of Six.

Grimmholder's gaunt cheeks, covered in a long, thick white beard filled one of the facets. On another side of the crystal was a very old looking dwarf man with hair and a beard as black as night, whose name was Trindelligrinian. Next to him was the face of a dwarf woman named Frinnwhizzle, also extremely aged. Her hair was reddish with streaks of silver and white, and unlike the claims of folktales, she did not have a beard. The last two faces were both elves, one male, the other female, and were siblings with hair as fine as silk and shiny as polished silver. The female's name was Bellagrinndihar, and her brother's was Jinndellihar.

"My brothers and sisters of the Order. I apologize for the late hour in which I have summoned you all," Hildegrinnel greeted.

"Make no apology, Hildegrinnel, as you well know the Order must always be vigilant," said Frinnwhizzle.

"It is very agreeable to see you. Have you located the Athenaeum?" asked Grimmholder.

"Yes, brother, I have." answered Hildegrinnel. "We would not have been successful if not for the warning from Jinndellihar."

"So there was something to what I told you?" asked Jinndellihar.

"There was, Jinn. Enchanted stone golems of immense size and strength, and a hunger to destroy. We were fortunate to defeat the vile behemoths. You were indeed correct, they were not intended to the protect the Athenaeum, but to prevent anyone from entering."

"And did you find any writings that would shed light on your quest?" asked Frinnwhizzle.

"There are no writings, Frinnwhizzle. The Athenaeum is a living entity of stone, in the image of a woman. She speaks as we do."

"That sounds amazing! I would be very grateful to see this Athenaeum in person!" exclaimed Trindelligrinian.

Hildegrinnel grimaced. "That is no longer possible, my friend. The Athenaeum was destroyed by the very individual that instituted the assassination of Lord Greggory Baylen."

"Who is the scoundrel?" Bellagrinndihar demanded, her pointed ears quivering in anger.

"His name is Bahraam of Revelstoke," Hildegrinnel answered.

None of the wizards or witches in the crystal knew of whom Hildegrinnel named, and their faces said as much.

"I was as confused as you are now, my

friends," began Hildegrinnel. "The Athenaeum revealed Bahraam was once the king of the Nine Isles."

"How can that be? History records that Richard Jaissen was the first king," declared Bellagrinndihar.

"After what I have witnessed, my friends, I can say that history is incorrect on this point," Hildegrinnel countered regrettably.

"If Bahraam is indeed the first king, he would have to be thousands of years old, would he not?" asked Bellagrinndihar.

"Yes, he would be over four thousand years old," Hildegrinnel guessed.

"What manner of creature is this Bahraam?" gasped Frinnwhizzle.

"He is what the Athenaeum called a gargoyle, and the power I witnessed in Skyvale, and here in Caledonia, is enough to give cause for urgency," Hildegrinnel explained. There was a brief silence while the Order digested her words.

"Do you know where Bahraam makes his home?" asked Bellagrinndihar calmly.

"He has none, Bellagrinndihar. The Athenaeum has said he is magically imprisoned, however, that prison is weakening. If Bahraam escapes, it could spell the destruction of this world."

A collective silence again fell over them and each face showed growing concern. Had they been told what was said by any other person, the Order would've shown skepticism, but the statement had come from Hildegrinnel, the most respected of all the Order. When she spoke, listening to her was always the best option.

"Can we repair the spell that holds him?" asked Trindelligrinian, the dwarf wizard of their group.

Hildegrinnel shook her head at him. "No my dwarf friend. Not even your unrivaled skill with spellmending can repair Bahraam's prison."

"It's obvious that someone cast the spell that imprisoned Bahraam. If we could learn the identity of the caster, perhaps we could find a descendant that may have in their possession the original spell," suggested Bellagrinndihar.

"Yes! I agree with Bellagrinndihar," said Trindelligrinian.

Hildegrinnel sighed. "That will not be necessary, my friends. I already know who the casters are."

"Casters?" asked Jinndellihar.

"Yes. We, the Order of Six, are responsible for Bahraam's imprisonment." Hildegrinnel told them, and the statement sent her brethren into stunned silence. "The Athenaeum said as much. We were the only ones, I believe, who were strong enough to do so."

"I have no memory of performing such an act," said Grimmholder.

"Nor do I," added Trindelligrinian and Jinndellihar.

Bellagrinndihar and Frinnwhizzle each nodded their affirmation of ignorance.

"None of us remember doing so," agreed Hildegrinnel. "We have grown very old, my friends, and have aged unnaturally, but we have not bothered to ask how or why."

"Exactly what are you trying to tell us, Hildegrinnel?" asked Bellagrinndihar.

"I am a human, and as we all know, humans do not live for hundreds of years. Yet I can remember a time when my face was youthful and my hair yellow as the sun, while at the same time dragons soared in the skies, but dragons have not been seen in the Nine Isles for over three hundred years. I should have passed a long time ago, but I have not," Hildegrinnel explained. "Trindelligrinian, Frinnwhizzle, as dwarves your race has a longer lifespan than a human, but still you cannot live for three hundred years, yet like myself and my brother, we have lingered on as though we were elves."

Jinndellihar and Bellagrinndihar, the only elves in the Order, both nodded in agreement.

"Do you think our involvement in Bahraam's imprisonment is responsible for our longevity?" suggested Frinnwhizzle.

"I believe so, but in what manner, I do not know. I think we have yet to learn the reason, but at the moment our concern is restoring Bahraam's prison, and I do not have all the information how to do so, but we do have one of the most important elements required…a dragon." Hildegrinnel said.

"How is that possible, sister?" asked Grimmholder.

"I do not know much more than she was in the Valley of Dayle since the disappearance of her kin," she explained.

"You have seen this dragon? Is it with you now?" asked Jinndellihar, peppering her with questions.

Hildegrinnel looked over her shoulder at Kaezanneth where she was now lying next to Rikter, still petrified like everyone else around the campfire. "She is."

"What else do we need to stop Bahraam's escape?" asked Grimmholder.

"We need a candidate to be king, and the spell that was originally cast."

"Can we speak to this dragon? Should we not verify that it is a dragon and not an imposter?" insisted Jinndellihar.

Hildegrinnel grimaced at his request. Why would he want to speak to the dragon and not take her word that a dragon was what she had met and allied herself with?

"She is no imposter, Jinn, she is what the Athenaeum called the Steward of Kings. It is her duty to choose a new king."

"How will she do this?" Frinnwhizzle asked.

"Again, I do not know. The Athenaeum was destroyed before I could learn anything further." Hildegrinnel informed them regrettably.

"I still would like to speak with this dragon at once!" Jinndellihar demanded quite adamantly.

Hildegrinnel cocked her head at Jinndellihar's aggressive attitude. For as long as she had known him, he had never made such a boisterous demand in spite of anything she ever said. Her word among the Order was taken with great respect and regarded as truth, requiring no proof other than her reputation for honesty.

"I will not disturb the dragon," she said, ironclad in her decision.

"Enough of this twaddle. It is late, Jinn," said Grimmholder, shutting down the tension rising between his sister and Jinndellihar. "We should end this conversation for now. I'm certain that what Hildegrinnel has told us about the dragon is truth. Allow the dragon and Lady Samarra's company to rest. They most certainly deserve a reprieve. Hildegrinnel, contact us when you have more to tell. May the Divines guide you."

The rest of the order wished Hildegrinnel well on her quest and the crystal went dark. The world around the witch then sprang to life. The moth fluttered around inside her tent, the fire on the candle danced wildly and those gathered around the campfire returned to their conversation and laughter as though nothing had happened. The wind again caressed the valley and the stars crawled across the blackened sky.

Hildegrinnel covered the crystal and returned to the campfire, her thoughts moving in a thousand different directions, but returning to a singular curiosity; why did Jinndellihar want to speak to Kaezanneth so badly? Why was her word not good enough for him?

TWO

Jinndellihar's crystal grew dark, the faces of the Order fading into nothingness as he covered it with a cloth. A sneer twisted the corners of his mouth while his jaw clenched tightly. Hildegrinnel had spurned him by ignoring his insistence of speaking to the dragon, and he disliked being told, not in exact words, no.

He struggled to stand, his knees and elbows creaking from extreme old age, and gestured with a hand as though he were grasping something. In a flash of warm light, like a candle flame, twin tendrils of living fire curled and corkscrewed from his palm, one end growing upward and ending in a perfect sphere where it shone like a marble-sized star. The other end flickered as it overlapped and stretched until it struck the polished marble floor of his chambers. The fire was his staff, and despite being made of fire, it neither burned him or the floor it touched, and emitted almost no heat.

Jinndellihar stepped out from behind the table where the crystal was, and lumbered across the spacious room, passing several shelves filled with old books and scrolls on one side, while on the other side were tables loaded down with more books, some opened and others stacked high. Ink wells and quills littered each table where they had been used to take notes on unrolled papyrus from those very old books. Lit candles burned, caked with melted wax that dripped down their length and dried at the base of each in clumps.

He passed into another part of his chambers where a large fireplace occupied one wall, oversized enough that a horse could've trotted into the fire inside. Against the opposite wall was an elegant, four post canopy bed lavishly adorned with thick blankets and the softest linens in Caledonia. He wanted to lay down and end the evening, but even with fatigue heavy upon his body he needed to do one task before allowing himself to rest.

With a wave of his hand the two floor to ceiling doors to his rooms swung inward at his command and he ventured into the corridor where he made his way through the royal palace of Dade. Royal guards dressed in silver and emerald colored armor stood at their posts throughout, nodding at his approach as he journeyed to the queen's wing. The floors and walls were the most beautiful granite to be found and were carved with curving patterns that seemed to go on forever, while the ceilings were three times the height of a man and vaulted.

Each lumbering step he took echoed throughout the castle. When he arrived at the entrance to the queen's apartments he was stopped by the Vanguard Knights, deadly warriors whose skill in combat had nearly no equal. Their task was only to protect the queen, and would die without hesitation.

Jinndellihar nodded at the captain of the Vanguards, Theurynndiel, a regal looking elf whose armor was decorated with a violet cloak hanging from his shoulders and held in place with a gold medallion engraved with the queen's seal, a silver sword ringed by an olive wreath.

"Jinndellihar, what brings you here at such a late hour? You are aware the queen is not to be disturbed once she has retired to her bedchambers?" said Captain Theurynndiel.

"I know this, captain, but what I have to tell her is more important than her precious 'beauty sleep'," snapped Jinndellihar.

"And just what might that be, wizard?"

Jinndellihar shot the captain a brazen glare. "I have found a dragon."

Captain Theurynndiel's expression fell and he stepped aside without another word.

Jinndellihar hurried to the end of the short corridor and knocked on the twin doors to Queen Brielle's chambers. He then opened the door with another wave of his hand like before in his own rooms, and went in without waiting for the queen to speak.

Unlike Jinndellihar's bedchamber, the queen's was twice the size and furnished with not only her oversized canopy bed draped in white satin linens, expensive sheets and the softest blankets in all the land, but also had several sofas and chairs of impeccable taste, along with a dozen grossly narcissistic statues, in her image, made of silver and gold. The fireplace was larger and contained a raging fire to combat the chill of the night. Wardrobes and dressers and tall mirrors lined one wall, while a large doorway into a wide closet housing an obscene number of dresses from all over the Nine Isles beset another wall. Hanging from the high vaulted ceiling was a gold and bronze chandelier, lit by fire-fairies trapped in decorative glass chalices.

The elf wizard went to the bed where Queen Brielle was sound asleep under the covers, and bent a knee before saying, "Your majesty, I need to speak with you."

Queen Brielle stirred and a hand went to her nearly pristine face that had age creases in her skin, a telltale sign of an elf reaching the elder phase of their lifespan. She brushed her long blonde hair, tinged with streaks of gray, from her forehead. She then went quiet.

"Your majesty," said Jinndellihar louder, "I need to speak with you!"

The queen murmured something and stirred. An eyelid rose and she peeked around for the noise that had rousted her. "Jinndellihar," she rasped. "Why do you disturb me, old man?"

"Believe me I would not have done so if what I had to say were unimportant," he said.

"For your sake, I hope so," threatened the queen.

Jinndellihar waited for the her to sit up but she remained at rest. "Would you like to rise, your majesty."

"Not until I have heard why you have interrupted my sleep," she told him. For her to sit upright at that moment was not something she was willing to do until she heard what he had to say.

"Prudent if I say so, your majesty."

"Get to it, Jinndellihar!" hissed the queen.

"As you wish. I can get you a dragon," he said, and no sooner had he said so, the queen sprang upright and looked upon him with her eyes that shone like two sapphires, blazing with a dark purpose.

"Where is this dragon!"

"It is with Hildegrinnel, from my order," he said.

"That does not tell me anything, old man!"

"I am aware of that, your majesty, but I have questions," Jinndellihar said. He had more than questions, he had demands. When he had come to Dade several years ago, he was looking for answers to his extreme aging, much like the rest of his brethren, and he assumed that if anyone had answers, it would be the elves, for they had a very long lifespan. Sadly, the elves he spoke with, many who were scholars at the university, had no answers for him.

He then sought an audience with Queen Brielle and impressed her enough to gain employ in her court, and was fortunate enough that she did need a wizard. Her previous prestidigitator had mysteriously disappeared many years ago, but he was certain that it was no mystery at all. The queen's reputation for cruelty and death knew no bounds.

What was very odd was that upon the second day of his employ, the queen had asked his council one evening, in secret, and set him to work immediately. What she had demanded so desperately that night, he could not do. She had shown him a scrap of parchment from a very old scroll, with a glyph emblazoned upon the papyrus. He studied the symbol for months upon months within the libraries of Dade and could find no meaning for the marking, that is until the queen gave him a peculiar, ragged journal written by an elf named Jothan.

Jinndellihar meticulously went through the small book page by page for endless nights, deciphering the writings. It was in that journal that he found the cryptic warning about the golems that he told Hildegrinnel about. It was also in that journal that he discovered the meaning of the glyph…

The symbol's meaning was a dragon.

Whatever the queen wanted, she needed a dragon to accomplish the task. When Jinndellihar told Queen Brielle what he had learned she was both ecstatic and enraged.

Dragons had vanished from the world centuries ago, and no one knew why they had gone, or where.

"I do not care for your questions, Jinndellihar! Tell me where the dragon is!" she commanded him furiously.

Jinndellihar rose and took a step back. His staff surged briefly, the flames sliding around his hand. "I will do what you ask, but only if you tell me why you need a dragon."

"This again?" the queen sighed. "I made it very clear when I employed you that my reasons for needing a dragon were my own!"

"That you did, your majesty, but I have decided to alter our relationship. I will not tell you without knowing your intentions."

The queen's attitude changed abruptly, and her eyes no longer flashed with anger. "I do not see what business it is of yours."

"Then I shall be on my way, your majesty. Good night," he said and turned to leave.

As he took a few steps, Queen Brielle leapt from the bed and rushed past to look at him. "What are your questions?"

"Ah, now you are interested in my questions, are you?"

"I may have been a little hasty." she admitted, her voice quivering. "What do you want to know?"

Jinndellihar stopped walking and gazed at her face. "Why do you need a dragon?"

The queen gasped with relief, feigned a smile, then told him…

THE STORY CONTINUES IN BOOK TWO,
THE CALAMITOUS QUEST
AND THE
TYRANT OF IRONSHIRE